"Have you ha...
visions, Elen...

She retreated from him, shaking her head as she tried to forget the vision she'd had that morning. Joseph opening her blouse, then her bra, staring at her breasts. Her heart pounded. "No."

"What did you see?" Joseph persisted.

Heat rose to her face, then moved lower, spreading throughout her body. She swallowed hard, reminding herself it was just a dream. "Nothing."

"You didn't act like it was nothing. You jumped when I touched you." His hand slid from her shoulder down her arm. She trembled as desire coursed through her. "Like now."

"Leave me alone, Joseph."

"You shouldn't be alone, Elena." His voice deepened to a sensual growl. "Was it *us*? Like this?" he teased, bringing her closer until her body brushed against the hard length of his.

"I'm not going to tell you." *I'd rather show you*. The wicked thought flitted through her mind, but she fought the temptation.

Joseph didn't. His head dipped, his mouth brushing across hers once, twice, before taking it in a deep, intimate kiss.

Dear Reader,

It's a thrill to be writing NOCTURNE books! I hope you're all enjoying this exciting new paranormal line!

Persecuted, my second book in the WITCH HUNT series, was a tough one to write because I identify so closely with the heroine, Elena, a mother desperate to keep her child safe. As every mother knows, that's not an easy task under normal circumstances, but Elena's matching wits with a madman intent on killing all witches. Not only does he know that Elena's a witch, he believes her young daughter is, too. Elena has to deal with her past, and accept who and what she is, as well as her future that comes to her in horrifying visions. Fortunately she has the help of her sister, Ariel (from *Haunted*), and her dream lover. While no white knight, by his own admission, Joseph's determined to protect her and her daughter. But can Elena convince him to love her, too?

I hope you enjoy Elena's emotional adventure in *Persecuted*.

Lisa

Persecuted

LISA CHILDS

MILLS & BOON
Pure reading pleasure™

All the characters in this book have no existence outside the imagination of the author, and have no relation whatsoever to anyone bearing the same name or names. They are not even distantly inspired by any individual known or unknown to the author, and all the incidents are pure invention.

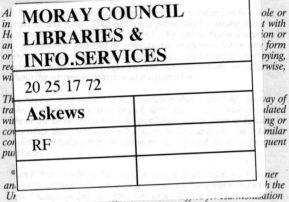

MORAY COUNCIL
LIBRARIES &
INFO.SERVICES

20 25 17 72

Askews

RF

First published in Great Britain 2008
by Harlequin Mills & Boon Limited,
Eton House, 18-24 Paradise Road, Richmond, Surrey TW9 1SR

© Lisa Childs-Theeuwes 2007

ISBN: 978 0 263 85990 4

46-0908

Printed and bound in Spain
by Litografia Rosés S.A., Barcelona

ABOUT THE AUTHOR

Award-winning author Lisa Childs wrote her first book when she was six, a biography...of the family dog. Now she writes romantic suspense, paranormal romance and women's fiction. The youngest of seven siblings, she holds family very dear in real life and her fiction, often infusing her books with compelling family dynamics. She lives in west Michigan with her husband, two daughters and a twenty-pound Siamese cat. For the latest on Lisa's spine-tingling suspense and heart-warming women's fiction, check out her website at www.lisachilds.com. She loves hearing from readers who can also reach her at PO Box 139, Marne, Michigan 49435, USA.

Chapter 1

The muscles in Elena's arms strained as she struggled against the ropes binding her wrists behind her back. Coarse fibers bit into her skin, scratching so deeply that blood, warm and sticky, ran down her wrists and pooled in her palms.

She bit her lip, holding in a cry at the sting. But that pain was nothing in comparison to the heat of the flames springing up around her. Sweat ran down her face, nearly blinding her, but still she could see a man on the other side of the flames. A hood covered his head; a dark brown robe concealed his body. But his frame, his height and the breadth of his shoulders, identified him as male.

Others stood behind him in the shadows and smoke, also clad in those dark brown robes. They chanted, their voices rising above the hiss and crackle of the flames.

"Exstinguo…veneficus…"

The words were unfamiliar but she suspected they called her a witch.

"Nooo…" She wasn't a witch. The smoke choked her, cutting off her protest and her breath.

Her line of vision shifted, away from the cloaked figures, to the woman bound to the stake in the middle of the circle of flames. *Was* Elena the witch? The woman's hair was dark and curly, not blond like Elena's. The woman's eyes were dark and wide, not pale blue.

Uncaring of the pain, Elena continued to struggle, trying to free herself from the hold of the ropes, of the dream. Of the vision.

A scream tore from her throat as she kicked at the covers and bolted upright in bed. Shaking, she settled into the pillows piled against her headboard and gasped for breath, her lungs burning.

As the woman was burning…

Even awake she could see her, illuminated by a flash of lightning inside Elena's mind. She squeezed her eyes shut and began a chant of her own: "It's just a dream. It's just a dream."

But she wasn't sleeping. She hardly ever slept

anymore for fear of dreaming of torture and murder. The images rolled through her mind no matter where she was or what she was doing. They weren't like the "dreams" she'd had her whole life, the innocuous images of something someone might do or say a day or two after she'd dreamt it. These weren't little revelations of déjà vu. They were murder, and she was an eyewitness to the unspeakable horror.

She reached out, needing the comfort of strong arms to hold her, to protect her. But for the blankets tangled around her legs, the bed was empty and cold. Her husband no longer shared their room. She'd been the one to throw out his stuff after accusing him of cheating. Not even his tyrant of a boss would send him out of town as often as Kirk was gone.

Truthfully, she'd been gone a long time, too. Despite the fact she'd rarely left the house, she'd been absent from their marriage. She'd pushed him away. But why hadn't he fought for her, for them? Had he ever loved her or only her money? The hurt that pressed on her heart wasn't new, like an ache from an old injury rather than a fresh wound.

She fumbled with the switch on the lamp beside the bed and flooded the room with light. Real light. Not that eerie flash only inside her head. The warm glow of the bulb in the Tiffany lamp offered no comfort, either.

Although he denied the cheating and only

moved as far as the guest room, she knew Kirk was lying, but she hadn't told him how she'd gained her knowledge of his affair. She'd "seen" him with another woman. At first she'd passed those images off as she had her others, figments of her overactive imagination or products of stress or paranoia. Finally she'd forced herself to face the truth about her sham of a marriage…and herself.

She didn't love Kirk; maybe she never had, because she'd never trusted him enough to tell him anything about her past or herself. During college their relationship had been mostly superficial and fun, things that Elena's life had never been. But their relationship had never really deepened, despite marriage, despite the beautiful four-year-old daughter they shared, and it had stopped being fun a long time ago. Sick of all the lies, his and hers, she'd finally filed for divorce.

For so long Elena hadn't been able to discern truth from fiction. Although she hadn't seen her mother in twenty years, she could hear her lilting voice echoing in her head with the words of a gypsy proverb, *There are such things as false truths and honest lies*.

When she'd been taken away from her mother two decades ago, she had also been separated from her younger half sisters. She'd only recently reconnected with Ariel. Elena had been twelve, Ariel nine and their youngest sister, Irina, just four when social services had taken them away from their mother. They'd never seen Mother again. Alive.

Ariel had seen her dead, though. Her sister could see people after they passed away. She hadn't wanted to see Elena and Irina for the first time in two decades the way she had their mother, so she'd searched for her sisters to warn them that someone had started a witch hunt. She hadn't found Irina yet, and had only stumbled across Elena by accident.

But Elena had already known about the witch hunt because of her dreams. She'd fought so hard to suppress her visions, to convince herself that they weren't real. When her sister had found her, Elena had had to admit to the truth, if only to herself.

The visions were why Elena was cursed, not the three-hundred-and-fifty-year-old vendetta that had started the first witch hunt. One of Elena's Durikken ancestors had been accused of killing the female members of the McGregor family and was burned at the stake. But like Elena, she'd seen her future and urged her daughter to run. That child, for whom Elena was named, had found safety, and she'd continued the Durikken legacy, passing on to her children the special abilities that people mistook for witchcraft.

Now someone else had resurrected the vendetta

that Eli McGregor had begun three and a half centuries ago, of ritualistically killing all witches. Elena had dreamed, sleeping and awake, of his murders. While she *saw* his victims, she hadn't seen the killer; she couldn't identify *him*. Helplessness and frustration churned in her stomach, gnawing at the lining like ulcers.

"I don't want this!" she insisted to the empty room, as she had for so many years.

Leaning over, she wrapped her fingers around the handle of the nightstand drawer and pulled with such force that the drawer dropped onto the floor. Papers flew out, scattering across the thick beige carpet. Her copy of the divorce papers. Her husband refused to sign his. She couldn't continue their farce of a marriage, which had been over long ago and was past time to officially end. If only she *was* a witch, like the legend claimed, then she could cast a spell on Kirk and make him go away forever. Somehow she suspected that a big check would do the job.

Elena rolled out of bed and dropped to her knees on the floor. Instead of picking up the papers, she pushed them aside. In the dim light, she couldn't see what she sought. Blindly she ran her fingertips through the carpet, raking it, until her nails grazed warm metal. She dug the pewter charm from the thick fibers, then dropped the little star, the tips dulled with age, into her palm. Twenty years ago her mother had pressed the star upon her, telling Elena that as well as keeping her safe, the charm would ensure that she never forgot who or what she was.

Images flashed in her mind like snapshots. A woman hanging. Another woman crushed beneath rocks. Another woman burning. Pain knotted her stomach and pounded at her temples. Her hands fisted, the points of the star digging into her palm.

She didn't want to remember those horrifying images.

She didn't want to be a witch.

She lurched to her feet and staggered to the bathroom. She lifted the lid to the toilet and dropped the little pewter charm into the water. Drops splashed up from inside the bowl, spattering the rim, as the star bobbed. Hand trembling, she reached for the handle. Maybe flushing the charm would stop the visions and make Elena normal. Her fingers closed around the metal handle, which was cool unlike the charm. The little star radiated warmth, always.

Her sister believed the charms held some special power to protect them, that if all three sisters united with the charms, they could stop the witch hunt. Elena's fingers slipped away from the handle. Then she reached into the bowl and pulled the star from the water. She'd held on to the charm too long to get rid of it now. Even though Elena didn't share Ariel's beliefs, she didn't want to shatter her sister's hope.

Her breath coming in shallow pants, she moved to the sink, turning on the gold-plated faucets to wash off the charm and her hands. Because of the soap, she kept a firm hold on the piece of metal, careful not to lose the star down the drain. She glanced at her image in the mirror, the disheveled blond hair, the wild light blue eyes, the silk chemise nightgown baring her shoulders.

"Liar," she called herself. She hadn't just lied to her sister when she'd claimed that the charms held no power; she had lied to herself, about so many things.

The marble floor cold beneath her bare feet, Elena walked from the bathroom. With one hand, she fitted the drawer back into the nightstand, then laid the star inside. The charm's warmth had already dried it, so it glistened in the soft glow of the Tiffany lamp.

Over the years Elena had many times considered tossing out the charm, but she always refrained. No matter how hard she'd tried to forget her past, a part of her had been unwilling to let go. With the witch hunt resurrected, that part would either prove her salvation…or her demise.

* * *

Elena had no idea how long she'd been asleep when moist lips touched her shoulder, gliding over the bare skin. Her pulse quickening, she murmured and shifted against the bed, struggling to awaken. She dragged in a deep breath, the scent of citrus soap and musk.

This was not her husband joining her in bed. He wasn't even down the hall tonight; he was out of town. But when he'd been around, he hadn't touched her, not for a long time. From the way he'd started looking at her, with uneasiness and a trace of fear, he might have figured out that his wife wasn't normal. Perhaps he'd picked up clues from her nightmares, or from the things she knew before he told her.

The lips moved, nibbling along her shoulder to her neck. The brush of moist, hot breath raised goose bumps along her skin. The blanket lowered, pushed aside by impatient hands. Then those strong, clever hands ran over her body, skimming down her arms, then around her waist and over her hips. Sometime during the night, even though the air blowing through her windows was cool in mid-May in western Michigan, she had removed her nightgown. Nothing separated her skin from his as his body brushed against hers.

"Elena," a deep voice whispered in her ear, his hot breath stirring her hair and her senses. "You're ready for me."

Excitement pulsed in her veins, and she opened her eyes, staring up into his face as he leaned over her. Desire had darkened his eyes so that only a thin circle of green rimmed his enlarged pupils. A muscle jumped in his cheek, shadowed with the beard clinging to his square jaw.

"Elena, I want you." His biceps bulged as he braced his arms on the mattress on either side of her, trapping her beneath the long, hard length of his body. His voice deepened to a throaty growl as he told her, "I want to bury myself so deep inside you that you'll feel me forever as a part of you."

"You're already part of me," she murmured.

His were the arms she'd instinctively sought earlier, when the horrifying dream had awakened her. She turned to *him* for comfort and protection. And for *this,* for the passion that pounded like a drum in her heart, heating her skin and melting her muscles so that she flowed beneath him, fitting herself to the hard lines of his body.

His chest tempted her, wide and muscular with soft, black hair that grew thinner as it arrowed down, over his washboard stomach. Some of the hair dusted his muscular legs, tickling hers, as he entwined them.

He was naked and ready. And so was she.

Her stomach quivering with anticipation, she reached up, twining her arms around his back, pulling him closer. But his weight didn't settle hot and heavy against her. Her arms moved through empty space, flailing the covers aside as she moved restlessly in her bed, empty but for her.

For the second time that night she bolted upright, panting for breath, her lungs burning with the struggle for air, as she awakened from a dream.

Just a dream.

This was no vision of the future, for there could be no future between Elena and her dream lover. Unlike the killer, she'd seen this man's face; she knew him, and wished she didn't.

He might not be the killer, but to Elena, he was just as big a threat, if not to her life, to her heart. His were the last arms in which she would find comfort or protection. With a man like him, she'd only find more heartache and danger.

Elena hadn't been to this wing of the house in six months, not since her father died. Each step on the Oriental runner that covered the wide corridor brought back more memories. Painful ones. That was one reason why she hadn't been back to this part of the Tudor mansion. She never wanted to relive those last weeks spent at her father's bedside, listening to his feverish ramblings as she watched him die.

Unlike the many times he'd taken ill before, this time the pneumonia had killed him. Maybe because he'd gotten it so many times before, or maybe because, as his mother had feared twenty years ago, he'd given up fighting for his life.

As with her visions, Elena had been helpless to stop his death. During his last days, half the time he'd thought she was her mother, so the fever had blinded him before killing him. She looked nothing like Myra Cooper with her wild curly black hair and big, dark gypsy eyes; eyes that had seen so much, like Elena's, through her visions. She might not have resembled her mother in looks, but Elena had taken after her in other ways.

The other half of the time, her father had thought she was *his* mother, which probably made more sense. She did resemble Thora Jones physically but in no other way. Elena still had her soul, even though she sometimes felt it slipping away… like when she had a vision of murder and didn't know how to prevent the killing.

Elena stood outside the door to her grand-mother's rooms, hesitant to knock. *She* was the other reason Elena had stayed away from this wing of the house. No good ever came out of contact with Thora Jones. The first time Elena met her paternal grandmother she'd been twelve and ripped away from her mom and sisters because of Thora's manipulations. Thora had sworn out the complaint that had declared Myra Cooper an unfit mother, causing the authorities to take away her children.

But Myra hadn't fought to keep Elena. She'd signed away her parental rights. Until Ariel had found her, Elena had thought she'd been the only one their mother had given up, because of who and what she was. But Myra hadn't kept any of her three daughters. Ariel believed it was because of the McGregor vendetta, that she'd been trying to protect them. Elena wasn't convinced. She was a mother; she couldn't imagine giving up her child for any reason but most especially if Stacia were in danger. No one would fight harder to keep a child safe than her mother.

That was why Thora had found Elena twenty years ago and brought her to this house, to give her son a reason to fight for his life. After a car accident paralyzed him, he'd wanted to die…until he'd met his daughter. He hadn't known about her existence until that day, but he'd immediately loved her. If not for her father, Elena wouldn't have stayed. She would have run away the first chance she got.

Growing up in this mausoleum had made Elena feel like a grasshopper trapped under a glass, powerless to escape and totally at the mercy of the person who held her captive. When she'd left for college, she had never intended to come back, but then her father had had one of his bouts with pneumonia. Thora had made certain Elena knew just how sick he was and how much he needed his daughter. So she'd been sucked back under the glass.

She curled her fingers into a fist but didn't lift it to knock. Not yet. Before she could, the door opened. "Elena."

Although she closed her eyes, she recognized the deep voice and wished for many reasons that she could disappear. Joseph Dolce wasn't her favorite person, probably because since her father died, he was her grandmother's favorite. Thora had trusted him enough, despite his relative youth and inexperience, to make him CEO of her corporation, stepping down herself from the position of power she had held since her husband died, from a heart attack, over twenty-five years ago.

Rumor was that Thora owned most of Barrett, the midsized city in the southwestern section of Michigan. Elena knew the rumor to be fact; she'd seen the business records since inheriting her father's shares of the company. Jones Inc. owned car dealerships, trucking companies, hotels and restaurants.

Now a thirty-five-year-old who'd grown up on the streets was in charge of the multimillion-dollar corporation. To his credit, Joseph had managed, despite some juvenile scrapes with the law, to go to college instead of prison. He'd also run a couple of those businesses under the Jones umbrella before running the whole thing. As Thora's CEO Joseph was at the house often, far too often for Elena's peace of mind.

"Mr. Dolce," she finally acknowledged him.

"Joseph," he corrected her. He'd been telling her to use his first name for the year since he'd become CEO, and she had yet to use it.

She probably never would. She didn't respect anyone who worked for her grandmother, even though at one time she'd used business to try to gain Thora's acceptance. When her father's health had compelled her to return, she'd asked Thora for a favor, the chance for some respect. But despite her MBA, her grandmother had refused to give her anything, let alone the role Elena had wanted running the company. She realized now that she'd been foolish to even ask, to give her grandmother more leverage with which to hurt her.

Her husband worked for Jones Inc., though, far beneath Thora and Joseph's level. Is that what had changed him from the sweet, fun-loving boy she'd met in college eleven years ago? Elena doubted

anyone could stay sweet and fun loving around
Thora, least of all someone as weak as Kirk.
Because he was weak, she couldn't fathom why
he had chosen to fight the divorce. Why now, when
she wanted him gone, did he refuse to leave?

She closed her eyes, as a headache nagged at her
temples. Her divorce was the least of her concerns
in light of her visions. The dissolution of her
marriage was trivial in comparison to someone's
life. Irina? Had her baby sister been the woman in
the fire in Elena's first dream the previous night?

She refused to think about her second, trying to
wipe it from her mind even as her body pulsed
with frustration in the way it had ended. Too soon.

"Elena, are you all right?" Strong fingers closed
around her arm, offering support.

Her heart lurched. Just with surprise, she told
herself. Joseph seemed more the type to shake
someone than hold her. Curiously enough she'd
always respected that about him, that he wasn't the
type to coddle anyone, that he was so strong that
he demanded strength from those around him.

When she opened her eyes, his head was close.
He had to be leaning, because he was tall, well
over six feet with wide shoulders and a chest so
muscular it strained the buttons on his gray shirt
and suit. His deep green eyes softened with
concern. Elena wasn't used to a man looking at her

like that, not since her father died. But underneath
the concern was something that unsettled her even
more, an awareness that hummed between them;
another reason she could never use his first name.
For them, it would be too intimate.

Like her dream.

She resisted the urge to tremble and lifted her
chin instead. "I'm fine."

"Yes, you are," he agreed, his voice deepening
with innuendo as he teased her. He always teased her.

Her palm itched to slap him. He didn't know
that she'd filed for divorce. She'd told no one yet.
For all he knew she was a happily married woman.
Didn't anyone respect marriage anymore?

Heat warmed her face, as an image from the
dream tugged at her memory. Arms and chest
rippling with muscles, wrapping tight around her,
pulling her close so that skin brushed skin. She
drew in a shuddery breath. But that had been just
a dream, not a vision. She was never going to
make love with *him*. She would make certain of
it, and if she could change that part of her future,
she could change more.

She was here, in her grandmother's wing,
because she couldn't keep ignoring her visions.
They weren't going away; they just kept getting
worse. Not for her, but for the people she saw in
them. She had to help. Like that ancestor who had

so long ago warned about the lightning that would cause the house fire and begin the vendetta, Elena had to take the risk—even if she was the one who wound up getting burned.

"Excuse me," she said, stepping around Joseph. "I need to speak to *her*."

Then she closed the door, shutting him into the hall and herself into her grandmother's rooms. The parlor, a profusion of Victorian roses and fragile, antique furniture, misled the visitor into thinking Thora Jones a delicate, old-fashioned woman. Nothing could be further from the reality.

Double doors led off the empty parlor into the den. Without knocking, Elena opened those doors into her grandmother's real sanctum: dark, heavy woods, dim light and the faint, lingering odor of pungently sweet cigars. Elena had never caught her smoking them, but she suspected it was one of her grandmother's many vices.

The woman lifted her gaze from the files on her desk, which was cluttered with more picture frames than work. Most of the photographs were of Elena's father, Elijah Jones. The only ones of Elena were snapshots taken with him. Thora's parlor also had several pictures of him, among the gardening ribbons and plaques, but this room with its faint light and solemn atmosphere felt more like a shrine to him.

This was where, since his death, Thora worshipped her son.

Elena turned her attention from the framed photographs to the woman behind the desk. Her grandmother's hair was as blond as Elena's, her eyes as eerily blue. Despite her seventy-three years, very few lines marred her pale complexion. Sometimes Elena wondered if her grandmother had sold her soul for beauty or immortality, but that thought was ridiculous.

Thora had sold her soul for vengeance.

Chapter 2

The older woman leaned back in her chair. But Elena suspected the nonchalance was feigned; tension emanated from Thora's trim body. "So…you're finally paying your grandmother a visit? How sweet." From her sarcastic tone, she considered it anything but.

So did Elena. "We need to talk."

Thora expelled an exasperated sigh. "I hope you're not going to bring up that foolishness of moving out again. It's your home, too. Your father saw to that in his will. And I think we've done very well these past six months at staying out of each other's way," she pointed out, then added, "until now."

"I'm not here to talk about moving out." Although she intended to, once her divorce from Kirk was settled, this house had never been *her* home. But she had something far more important than moving to discuss. Because Elena had yet to tell her grandmother about Ariel, because she wasn't certain that she should, she said, "I have to find *them*."

To her credit Thora didn't ask *who*, even though they hadn't had this conversation for a long time, since Elena was a girl desperate to be reunited with her mother and half sisters. "Not this again."

"You know where they are." Thora knew everything. Sometimes Elena wondered if she, too, was cursed. In a way, she supposed Thora was, but her special abilities were money and power. The only problem was she would never have enough of either to make her happy. The money couldn't buy her happiness; it hadn't even been able to save her only child.

"What's brought this on? Is this about your father?" Thora asked.

So much of the past twenty years had been about her father. He'd been sick for so long his death should have been a relief, but Elena still ached for missing him. She shook her head. "No."

"You're missing him so much that you want to find some other family now," Thora speculated. "They're not your family, Elle."

"They're my sisters, and I need to find them." An image flashed through her mind, of the curly dark-haired woman tied to a makeshift stake, of flames rising up around her, swallowing her as she was trapped in the middle, screaming. Even though pain hammered at her temples, she raised her voice, shouting, "Now!"

Thora's eyes widened with surprise over Elena's vehemence. Then her mouth twisted into a patronizing smile. "You aren't a little girl anymore, Elle. It's past time you grow up and realize they won't want to see you. You're the reason they were split up, that they grew up in foster homes. They know that, and they must hate you for it."

She'd heard this first when she was twelve; it hurt no less now, all these years later. But she wasn't a child anymore. She could hold back the tears and hide the pain, but she'd done that even at twelve, convincing herself that Thora lied to her, that her mom and sisters were still together. Lying to herself was smarter than showing her grandmother any sign of weakness; instinctively she'd known that then. That, like so many other things, hadn't changed over the past twenty years.

Drawing on her strength and pride, Elena lifted her chin and revealed, "Ariel doesn't hate me."

The color drained from Thora's face. "You've already found one of them?"

"She found me." By accident. She'd actually been looking for Thora, to confront the person who'd sworn out the complaint that had separated their family. Elena would make certain that meeting never happened. She didn't want her grandmother treating Ariel the way she'd treated Elena, with resentment and bitterness at their mother.

"If she's talking to you now, it's only because she doesn't know everything. Yet." Thora shook her head, as if she pitied Elena, but a small, satisfied smile played around her mouth. "Maybe I should enlighten her."

"No." Ariel deserved to know the truth, but Elena was the one who needed to tell her. Not Thora. Twenty years ago Elena hadn't been able to protect her sisters from Thora's manipulations, but now she was older and wiser. She wouldn't let Thora hurt them again.

The older woman threatened, "I will tell her some *interesting* family secrets, if you don't drop this now. If you don't stay away from them."

"*She* is my family. I have a right to speak to her. And Irina." Again the vision flashed into her mind, in a bright beam of light, the woman trapped in the middle of the flames. Instead of cigars, Elena caught the odor of wood smoke; it burned in her nostrils, the image was so real. "I need to find Irina."

Thora's blue eyes flickered, the first sign of genuine annoyance. "Those women are *nothing* to you anymore. They never were. Accept that."

Frustration clutched at Elena's throat, making it hard for her to draw a breath. She wanted to scream, to throw things. But she restrained all those urges. She'd learned well how to control herself the past twenty years. She could restrain her passion and her temper—but not the visions. She'd never learned how to *control* her ability, only how to *deny* it.

Thora sighed. "I can't believe how ungrateful you are. I saved you from that life, from that hand-to-mouth existence and brought you here, to live in luxury, with a father who loved you."

She never claimed to love Elena though. If not for how devoted she'd been to her son, Elena would have thought Thora incapable of love. But was that obsessive devotion to Elijah, like when she'd deliberately broken up Elena's family, really love or something darker?

As dark as the man who lurked in the shadows of Elena's visions, his face obscured but his intentions clear?

She ignored her grandmother's diatribe. She had come to reason with Thora, not argue. "Ariel found me because we're in danger. We need to find Irina, to warn her, too."

Thora shook her head as her thin lips twisted with disgust. "I thought you were smarter than that. How much money did Ariel want for this information? How much were you foolish enough to pay her?"

"She doesn't want my money."

Ariel was probably one of the few people to whom wealth meant nothing. She cared only about protecting the sisters she hadn't seen in so many years. With her determination, it was only a matter of time before she learned everything, like Thora had said, all the family secrets. Elena couldn't put off telling the truth any longer.

The older woman laughed, the sound of it forced and brittle. "Stupid little girl—"

"She's telling the truth." Elena defended her sister, as she should have defended them and their mother two decades ago. She should have insisted that Thora reunite the family she'd destroyed.

But in Thora's mind, she'd done the right thing by having the children taken away from Myra Cooper. She'd insisted that they were better off away from their mother. She'd relished pointing out how Myra had given up her parental rights to Elena.

Elena swallowed hard, then revealed, "Before Ariel found me, I *knew* we were in danger."

"How would *you* know that?" Thora asked, with more than annoyance in her blue eyes now, an almost indiscernible trace of fear, the same fear Kirk couldn't quite hide whenever he looked at her. He had to know. He must have figured out exactly *what* he'd married.

Elena drew in a deep breath. Maybe it was better, for all of them, that they knew. She couldn't deny the visions any longer, not to herself or anyone else. "I just *know*."

"You're talking that crazy stuff again." The older woman stood up now and thumped a fist on her desk, scattering papers across the surface as the picture frames rattled. "You will not bring that witchcraft into my home. Do you understand me?"

Elena flashed back, not to a vision or a dream, but to a memory two decades old. The first time she'd told her grandmother of a vision she'd been subjected to a similar tirade. Then she'd been sent to counseling and therapy and prescribed drugs to treat her "disorder." The doctors and therapists had claimed it was everything from separation anxiety to post-traumatic stress, blaming everything on her mother, like Thora always did. She hated that her son had fallen in love with Myra Cooper.

"I understand you," Elena said, knowing that the hatred had consumed whatever decency her grandmother might have had. Elena would get no help, from Thora Jones, in locating Irina. "You've never understood *me*. So let me go—"

"Go, get the hell out of here, if that's the way you want it," Thora said, shaking with rage. She picked up one of the framed photos from her desk and turned the picture toward Elena. From her grandfather's arms, a little blond girl smiled sweetly at them. "But *she* stays."

Elena's heart clenched with love and fear. "You can't take away my daughter."

"Funny, I think that's exactly what your mother told me."

Her grandmother's laughter echoed in her ears, as Elena rushed out of her rooms. She slammed the door to the corridor, then sagged against it, squeezing her eyes shut on the image of Thora's hateful face. Every confrontation with her grandmother left Elena this way, weak, shaking…with a little less of her soul.

"Are you all right?"

She opened her eyes, confronting Joseph's concerned gaze again. "You stayed."

He nodded, those deep green eyes soft again with sympathy. "Things never go well between you and your grandmother."

"So you thought what?" She lifted a brow, relieved to feel anger, which made her so much stronger than fear. "That I might need you?"

Haughty, scornful—she'd rather Joseph see her that way than weak. Like Thora, he wouldn't respect weakness. But why did she want his respect? He was too much like her grandmother. That was why he'd been given the job that by birthright should have been hers. But refusing to hire her had been more favor than punishment for Elena. If she'd worked for Thora, she might have begun to act like her as well, and she never wanted to become that hateful, bitter and unscrupulous.

"I tend to forget that you hate me," he said, his wide mouth quirking into a wicked grin.

So did she. That scared her nearly as much as her grandmother's threats, which weren't empty. She had enough money and power to get whatever she wanted. Not that she especially wanted Stacia. She just wanted to manipulate Elena. Since she couldn't do it through Elena's father anymore, she would do it through Elena's daughter.

Elena did understand the older woman. She understood that Thora couldn't let her son go despite his death. She needed more than the pictures piled on her desk and adorning every wall of her rooms. Because Elena and Stacia were part of him, she wanted to keep them close even though she hated that Elena was also a part of her mother, and had been punishing Myra through her since the day she'd brought Elena to this house.

Joseph stepped close, the sleeve of his suit brushing against the silk of her blouse. Even through the two layers of material, his heat penetrated, raising her temperature. Her face flushed. She would have stepped away, but her back was against the door. And he towered over her, imposing, intimidating.

Was this why her grandmother had hired him? Because just his presence, his brawn and the breadth of his shoulders and chest, was threatening? Elena suspected the greater threat was the sharp intelligence burning in his green eyes.

"Why do you hate me, Elena?" he asked. His voice, deep and soft, lifted the hair on the nape of her neck. His wicked grin never slipped, amusement lightening his eyes.

Damn him, he *knew.* She *wanted* to but couldn't quite hate him, no matter how much she tried. She opened her mouth, ready to list the reasons, some she'd vented before, like his subordinates sending her husband away on business too much. But that had been more help than hardship. She'd realized that absence hadn't made her heart grow fonder, only Kirk more faithless. She couldn't blame Joseph for that, since Kirk didn't work directly under him. She couldn't even blame Joseph for the dreams.

All she could do was ask, "*Why* do you work for her?"

Was it blackmail? Like what kept Elena in this house, the threat of her grandmother using the considerable means at her disposal to take away what mattered most to Elena, her daughter? What was Thora holding over Joseph Dolce? What mattered most to this man?

He shrugged, and his arm moved against hers, wool scraping against silk. "Money. She pays me well."

"To do her dirty work," Elena scoffed, inexplicably disappointed that he wasn't being coerced, too. This was why she had to hate him, why she could never trust him. He was just as soulless and manipulative as his employer, willing to do whatever necessary for money and power. "I hope it's enough."

His dark head nodded, but his green eyes dimmed, the amusement gone. "It's a lot of money, more than I ever really thought a kid who grew up like I did could make." Wistfulness deepened his voice. "I used to dream about the fast cars, big houses and fancy—" the wicked grin flashed a brief appearance as he stared down at her "—women."

He considered her a fancy woman? On the

outside, she might look the part of an heiress, with the silk clothes and sleek hairdo and manicured nails. Inside, she was still that little girl who'd grown up in the back of a truck camper, eating cold canned food and wishing for a hot shower and a soft bed, one she hadn't had to share with younger sisters who kicked and flailed elbows in their sleep. Guilt nagged at her, as it had twenty years ago, when she'd thought her wishing had caused her mom to lose her and her sisters. She'd gotten her hot shower and soft bed, but she hadn't been able to sleep in it for a long time. She'd missed her sisters, flailing elbows and feet, too much.

"So you got what you wished for," she pointed out to Joseph, but for some reason she suspected he wasn't any happier than she'd been. "Was it worth it, selling out to Thora?"

She had no doubt the older woman made him do things, probably illegal things, to get her what she wanted for her corporation and herself. Perhaps that was another reason why Thora hadn't hired her; she'd known Elena would have wanted to run the company honestly.

Irritation darkened his eyes. "You can act all sanctimonious and self-righteous," he accused. "You don't have a damn clue how it is growing up with nothing—"

"I've been poor," she interrupted him. But she

hadn't had nothing. She'd had her mom and her sisters. Their love. She swept an arm around the wide corridor full of antiques and framed artwork. "And obviously I've been rich. I was much happier poor."

He stepped even closer, his legs brushing hers, only inches separating his chest from hers. She could nearly feel the beat of his heart beneath his wool suit and silk shirt. She lifted her palms, wanting to push him away. But she dropped her hands back to her sides and fisted them, not trusting herself to touch him…because she couldn't trust him.

Interest narrowed his green eyes as he studied her. "There's a helluva lot I don't know about you, isn't there?"

"More than you could handle," she admitted.

"That sounds like a challenge," he said, the amusement back in his wicked grin and sparkling eyes, as he lifted her chin with the pad of his thumb.

He stroked her skin, which until that moment Elena had never known was so sensitive. She bit her bottom lip, resisting temptation. Then she lifted her fists, using them to shove against his chest so she could step away from the door and away from him.

"I've never backed down from a challenge, Elena," he warned her, as she walked away.

If he learned the truth, would he look at her like

Thora did? Like Kirk had started to look at her, when he dared meet her eyes?

Like she was crazy.

God, she wished she was, then she wouldn't have to worry about her visions, any of her visions, coming true.

Elena sat up in bed, her back sinking into the pillows piled against the brass headboard. A book lay open across her bent knees, but she couldn't concentrate on the words on the page, swimming in and out of focus. She was so tired but too afraid to sleep…for the dreams she might dream.

Tomorrow she would talk to Ariel. Together, they would find their little sister. They would make sure none of Elena's visions of Irina came true. With that thought giving her some peace, she drifted off to sleep…until a cry awoke her. For once, it wasn't hers, drawn out by a horrifying vision.

She threw back the blankets and ran the short distance down the hall to Stacia's room, which was aglow with ambient light from the Strawberry Shortcake lamp next to the little girl's bed.

"Sweetheart," she murmured, pulling the little girl into her arms. "It's okay. Shhh…"

Stacia hiccupped out a soft sob and burrowed against her mother. "Daddy…" she called out sleepily.

Elena brushed her daughter's blond curls off her damp forehead. "It's okay, honey. Mommy's here."

The same could not be said of Daddy. Elena knew she'd done the right thing, taking the first step to end her sham of a marriage, for her daughter's sake. If Mommy and Daddy no longer lived together, she would understand why he was never around, instead of her confusion giving her nightmares. She rocked the warm little body in her arms as Stacia snuggled against her.

"Where's Daddy?" the little girl asked.

No doubt in another woman's bed. But she couldn't tell her daughter that. "He's away, honey. Remember? He had a business trip."

Stacia rubbed her eyes, which were the same pale blue as Elena's and Thora's. "I saw him in my dream," she said.

Of course she had to dream about the man; he was never around. Why wouldn't he just sign the papers and officially end their marriage? Elena suspected he'd grown too accustomed to their big house and his fast cars and didn't want to give them up. He'd worked with Thora and Joseph too long.

"Did you dream about your daddy, honey?" she asked. At least when Kirk was around, he played with Stacia. He wasn't the most devoted father, but he could be fun, playing silly games with their little girl. Too bad he was playing games with Elena, too.

"He was with somebody, Mommy. And then—" she shuddered "—something bad happened…"

The fine hair on the nape of Elena's neck lifted as foreboding washed over her. Her daughter couldn't be talking about a vision. She couldn't be cursed, too. Elena ignored the little voice in her head, reminding her of the Durikken legacy passed from generation to generation.

"What happened, Stacia?" she asked.

Small shoulders lifted in a jerky shrug as fear thickened her voice. "I dunno…I was hiding…"

"It was just a dream, sweetheart." It had to have been. Her daughter couldn't be cursed, too.

But if not for the vendetta, perhaps having visions wouldn't be a curse. Through them Elena had learned what man to divorce…and what man to resist. If not for the killer continuing the vendetta, she wouldn't be having visions of murder.

"Let me read you a story," she told Stacia, asking nothing more about her daughter's dream. She'd like to think she was doing it to avoid upsetting Stacia any further, but it was probably herself she didn't want to upset. Denial was her oldest, closest friend; she had preferred it to counseling and anti-hallucinatory drugs.

She picked up a book from the table beside the

bed. Even though she was only four, Stacia could read most of the words in her books, or maybe it was just that she memorized them from Elena having read them to her so many times. Either way, she was one smart little girl.

Elena pulled her daughter close and opened the book across her lap. She read of princesses and glittery white unicorns, but in her head, she didn't see those images.

Elena didn't see Kirk, like Stacia had. She saw a woman with dark, curly hair. The woman from the fire. She was young, only in her early twenties, but she appeared to have lived hard. She was dirty, wild-eyed, staggering along a back alley…until a man stopped her, his arms reaching out of the shadows to grab her.

Elena jerked, and Stacia murmured a protest at the sudden movement. "Shh…" she said, soothing her daughter and trying to soothe herself.

She'd had this dream before, but she couldn't make sense of all her visions. They came to her in no particular order, some flashing through her head time and time again. She'd seen many images of this woman who might be Irina; dirty, unkempt, probably homeless. Was that where the man found her little sister, in an alley, all alone?

Her arms tightened around Stacia's warm body. Although her daughter looked nothing like her, she reminded Elena of Irina. Her baby sister had been only Stacia's age when they were separated.

"It's okay, Mommy," Stacia murmured in her sleep, the child offering comfort to the mother. "You'll find her…"

Elena tensed. How did Stacia know what she was thinking? Had she…

No, she must have overheard some of Elena's conversations with Ariel. She must have learned about their search for Irina through things Elena had let slip. She wasn't cursed. She was just an in-sightful child, like Irina had been. At four she'd had that uncanny ability, too, to figure out what someone was thinking.

What was she like now, as an adult? Was she even still alive? They had no proof. Although Ariel saw ghosts, they usually didn't seek her out unless they knew her. Did Irina even remember them? She'd been so young….

Guilt nagged at Elena. She should have tried to find her sisters before the killing started. She should have been stronger than Thora's threats and manipulations. She had to put aside the guilt and fear now, if she was going to be strong enough to stop a killer, and protect her sisters.

The old brick mansion loomed on the other side of the wrought-iron gates, illuminated by security lights, guarded and impenetrable. Maybe to others but not *him*. He could get inside whenever he was ready, tonight, under the cover of the shadows where he stood now just outside the fence or tomorrow, in broad daylight.

A light, tinged with red, shone faintly in a third-story window. The little girl's room, but the silhouette of a woman moved behind the frilly curtains. They were there, together. Two of the witches. Mother and daughter.

Could she sense his presence? Did she know he stood below her daughter's window? Or wasn't that how her witchcraft worked? What was Elena's special ability? Was she like her mother and could see the future? Or was she like her sister who saw ghosts?

One of them could hear people's thoughts. He knew this because when he'd killed their mother, her memories had become his. He'd relived the moment when she'd given them up, bestowing upon each of them a charm before letting them go. He couldn't quite remember who had which ability though.

Was Elena the telepath? Could she read his mind? Did she know what he was planning? He needed to kill one of them to renew his strength. To keep going until he could reclaim the charms and deal with them all.

Pain throbbed in his shoulder and at his temples,

stealing his strength. He didn't know what hurt worse, the inoperable tumor growing in his head or the wound where the redheaded witch had shot him. His knees wobbling, he reached for the fence and twined his fingers around the iron spires, holding himself up.

Not tonight but soon, before he weakened any more, he had to kill one of the witches. With her death, he would regain some power he lost because of the redhead. Because of her, he'd lost the cult of followers he'd formed to help with the witch hunt. He'd been forced to abandon his church, but he didn't need it or the cult. After killing another witch, he would be strong enough to take on the other witches, alone, and reclaim the charms that rightfully belonged to the McGregors. He needed the magic of the charms to restore his health.

He'd decided on the witch he needed to kill next—the only one he was strong enough now to kill on his own.

Did Elena know that he intended to kill her daughter?

Chapter 3

"I'm glad you called," the redhead said, walking at Elena's side along the cobblestone paths winding through the elaborate gardens on the estate. Even though she didn't physically resemble their mother, either, Ariel dressed like a gypsy in her long gauzy skirts and laced-up peasant blouses; so different from Elena's conservative attire of cream-colored linen skirt and sleeveless silk blouse.

"Did you finally talk to your grandmother? Does she know where Irina is?" Ariel asked.

Elena's focus remained on the flowers, the

fragrant blossoms in myriad colors, brilliant blues, blazing reds as well as an array of yellows, pinks and purples. The gardens had won awards for beauty. Her grandmother displayed the ribbons in her parlor, taking the credit when all she'd done was hire the best landscapers, the hardest-working gardeners. As Thora often boasted, she hired only the best, like Joseph. At just the thought of him, Elena's pulse jumped, her face heating.

"Elena?" Ariel nudged her with an elbow. "So did you talk to her?"

She nodded in response to her sister's impatient question.

Ariel uttered a little scream of frustration. "So tell me, does she know where Irina is?"

"No, and I actually believe her. She thought Irina had gone into foster care, like you had."

Ariel had been bounced from home to home because of the curse, because every time she admitted to seeing dead people, her foster parents thought she was crazy and either shipped her off to another family or a psychiatric facility.

Guilt tied Elena's stomach into knots. Ever since Ariel had found her, she'd struggled to meet her younger sister's turquoise gaze, not just because of what her grandmother had done but who she was.

Ariel's brow wrinkled as she narrowed her eyes.

Her voice soft, she observed, "There isn't a lot of love between you and your grandma."

"You don't understand." Elena dreaded explaining, but her sister deserved to know the whole truth, all of the family secrets.

An arm slid around her shoulders as her sister half embraced her, bumping her hip against Elena's. "I know," she said.

Ariel couldn't know everything; she only knew that Thora had been the one to report Myra. Elena pulled away, unable to accept her sister's affection until she'd told her everything.

"What do you think you know?" she asked Ariel, whose turquoise eyes softened with sympathy.

"I can see that you didn't have it any easier than I did growing up, maybe even harder," Ariel commiserated.

"I had my dad," Elena said, not bothering to claim her grandmother. "He loved me…until he died six months ago."

"I'm sorry," Ariel said, lifting her arm again but instead of embracing her sister, she brought it back against her side.

Regret over rebuffing her sister twisted Elena's stomach, along with the grief she still felt over losing her dad. "He'd been sick a long time."

Ariel began again, "I'm sorry—"

But Elena waved off her sympathy. She

wouldn't bother Ariel with the details about his health. She had something more relevant to tell her. "His name was Elijah."

Ariel stopped walking, her long, slim body taut and still. "It was?"

"It's a family name they kept using even though my father's ancestors changed their last name years ago, when they first came to America." That was why Ariel's search for McGregor descendants who may have resumed the vendetta hadn't turned up Thora. Or Elena. She'd found Thora only through the complaint sworn out against their mother.

Ariel's eyes widened, the turquoise the only color in her pale face. "What are you saying?"

From her sister's reaction, Elena was pretty certain that she'd figured it out. "My grandmother is a descendant of Eli McGregor. She named her son after him."

"After the man who killed our ancestor, burning her at a stake." Ariel's voice cracked with emotion. Their mother had died the same way. Burned.

While Ariel could see her ghost, Elena had witnessed the murder…in a vision. She blinked back tears, saddened that she would never have the chance to see her mother again.

"So you're a McGregor." Ariel expelled a

shaky breath, stirring the red hair that had fallen across her cheek.

Pride lifted Elena's chin. "And a Durikken."

Ariel sighed. "I've been trying to find McGregors, trying to figure out which one of them might have resurrected the vendetta."

"You think *I* could be the killer?"

Ariel studied her, as if assessing her older sister's strength. Then she shook her head, tumbling her hair around her shoulders. "No."

Elena's pride stung; her sister hadn't sounded convinced. "Are you sure? After all you really don't know me. Until just a couple weeks ago we hadn't seen each other in twenty years."

A little chuckle sputtered out between Ariel's lips. "Do you *want* me to think you're the killer?"

"No. I want you to really *believe* that I'm not."

"You're right. We haven't seen each other since we were kids, but I know you, Elena. You're incapable of murder." Ariel's turquoise gaze lifted toward the house.

Elena suspected she didn't seek her niece's bedroom window. She'd never invited her sister inside, so Ariel would have no way of knowing which wing was Elena's and which Thora's. Elena wanted her sister to have no contact with the bitter old woman. If not for Stacia having been tired from her fitful night, Elena would have taken her along to meet Ariel at the playground where they'd met before.

"What about your grandmother?" Ariel asked.

"Her family changed their name from McGregor because they considered Eli McGregor a madman who should have been punished for what he'd done—"

Bitterness hardened Ariel's voice when she interrupted, "But the townspeople had revered him for killing a witch."

"Or feared him," Elena said. "He was crazy. The vendetta was crazy, and his children changed their name because they wanted no part of it."

But she couldn't say the same of Thora, not and believe it. Her grandmother claimed she'd only taken away Myra's daughters because she was an unfit mother, but Elena had always suspected something other than concern for the children or love of her son had motivated Thora's actions. Vengeance.

"*None* of her family wanted anything to do with the vendetta?" Ariel asked.

"My father was her only son." Perhaps that was why her love for him had bordered on obsessive. Did Elena love Stacia like that, so much that she shut out everyone else? Kirk had excused his absence by claiming that Elena had no room in her life for anyone but her daughter and her father. Not her husband. He might have been right, but Elena hated to think she was more than just physically like her grandmother.

"And your father's dead," Ariel concluded, then shook her head. "It's all so incredible. How'd a McGregor hook up with a Durikken? Coincidence?"

Elena glanced toward the house, not the wing where her daughter slept, hopefully, a dreamless slumber, but toward her grandmother's wing. She hoped her parents' meeting had been just a coincidence. She bit her lip, then released it to sigh. "My father was a good man. A loving man. He wouldn't have sought our mother out to hurt her."

Ariel's lips lifted in a wistful smile. "Maybe he only wanted to apologize for what his family had done to hers all those years ago. And when they met, they fell in love."

Cynicism forced Elena to point out, "It didn't last." Not with the conflict and obstacles they'd had. She glanced again toward the house, to the shadow looming behind the gauzy curtains in her grandmother's parlor.

Ariel's head turned as she followed Elena's gaze to the house. "So there's only you and her?"

"And Stacia." But Elena had an uncomfortable feeling her daughter was mostly Durikken, cursed.

Frustration knitted Ariel's forehead. "But maybe your grandmother has some distant relatives. You have to ask her."

"She's not going to help me. She doesn't believe that we're in danger."

"Did you tell her about our aunts?" Like their mother, they had been murdered. But unlike Myra, their bodies had been found. Ariel had found them, hanged and crushed to death.

"Thora doesn't want to believe that someone started up the witch hunt again."

Ariel sighed. "Because then she'd have to accept that one of her relatives, no matter how distant, is a killer."

"You don't know for certain that a McGregor is behind this," Elena felt obligated to point out.

"Who else would resume the vendetta but a McGregor? Who else would even know about it?"

Elena's shoulders ached as if a weight had settled on them. "You're probably right."

Ariel reached out again, despite all the times Elena had pulled away from her, and squeezed her shoulder. "You can't blame yourself for this, just like you can't blame yourself for Thora swearing out that complaint against Mama."

Perhaps her sister knew Elena better than she'd realized despite her guilt causing her to keep Ariel at arm's length. "I don't—"

Ariel interrupted the denial with a shake of her head. "You can't help who your family is, who you are. You just have to accept it."

And that was what Elena struggled with the most, accepting her ability and her conflicting heritage. "That's easier said than done."

The redhead bobbed in a commiserating nod. "Do you have any visions of your own death, Elena?"

"I don't know." She rubbed her hands over her bare arms, trying to chase away the chill, but it wasn't on her skin; the cold was deep inside her. "Sometimes when I'm dreaming, it's like it's me who's being killed. Then I step back, and I see that it's someone else."

Her voice flat, matter-of-fact, Ariel acknowledged, "Me."

"Or Irina. I've seen Irina."

Ariel remembered, "On the streets."

Images of her most recent vision played through her mind. "He catches her."

Ariel's eyes widened with shock and dread. "Oh, God!"

"And I think he kills her the way he killed Mother." Unless the image of the woman burning at the stake had been the memory of the vision of her mother dying. The woman had looked exactly like their mother. Unlike Ariel, who had accepted her ability as a gift, Elena struggled to even understand hers.

"We have to find our baby sister."

"I want to help you," Elena said. But she didn't

know how to use her ability, not unless the vision was really clear, and that had only happened once, when the killer had nearly ended Ariel's life. Elena had noted the details of the dilapidated church where Ariel, her fiancé, David, and his friend, Ty, tracked the killer and his cult. But Ty had been hurt, and the killer had gotten hold of Ariel, tying a noose around her neck. David had gotten her away from the madman, but he'd been stabbed. If not for Ariel shooting the killer, David probably would have died. Thankfully they'd all survived. Regrettably, so had the killer, who'd gotten away.

That night, seeing Ariel and David's love for each other, had forced Elena to face the reality of her loveless marriage. She hadn't even told Kirk about her sister finding her.

Ariel began, "If you want to help me—"

"I do!" Elena insisted.

"Then you have to accept yourself, Elena, *everything* about yourself."

Elena's lips pulled up into a reluctant smile. "I thought you were a teacher, not a psychiatrist."

Her sister shrugged. "I guess I must have picked up something from all the ones who talked to me when I was growing up, who tried to pass my gift off as a bid for attention, or a coping mechanism for losing my family."

While her grandmother had had harsher explanations, a few counselors had told Elena the same things about attention and coping. Softly she acknowledged, "Maybe they were right."

"You don't believe that I see ghosts?"

"Our mother was a con artist who staged séances to bilk people out of money." Until they'd been taken away from her, they'd helped.

Maybe that was why Elena was drawn to Joseph; she wasn't so different from him. She knew how it was to be a kid forced to do whatever necessary to survive. But she'd grown up and realized there were better ways. Someday, maybe, so would he.

She sighed. "I don't know what to believe."

Instead of taking offense, her sister chuckled. "That was crazy. Mama had more gifts than you and I. She didn't have to lie to them, but she thought lies made them happier than the truth."

"There are such things as false truths and honest lies." Her mother's favorite gypsy proverb.

Ariel nodded. "You remember that, too. Remember who you are. Then you can help me." Her heels clicked against the cobblestone path as she left Elena standing alone in the middle of the garden, trying to absorb her sister's ultimatum.

Ariel could accept that her sister was a McGregor, but she didn't want Elena's help until she'd accepted herself? Her ability, her heritage or both? Either way, she asked the impossible. But to find Irina, to save her sisters from a killer, Elena would find the strength to conquer the impossible.

She glanced toward the four-story house again, her gaze focusing on the windows of her grand-mother's parlor where behind the gauzy curtains the shadow loomed, watching her. Always watching her, worried about her well-being, as she'd claimed when Elena was twelve, or planning her destruction?

"Why are you here?" Elena asked Joseph as she opened the door to his handsome face.

She stepped back as he shouldered his way into her private living room. The room was bigger than most modest ranch houses, with a massive, sand-stone fireplace on the outside wall, in the middle of a row of leaded glass windows. The walls were a soft pale blue, with trim and furniture in chocolate brown and rich cream. An ornate oak staircase wound up opposite the door to the hall of the main house, the door through which Joseph had pushed his way.

"Do you need to talk to Kirk?" she asked, un-settled by his physical appearance as much as his visit. She didn't even know if Kirk was back from his last trip, but then Joseph would probably know before she would. Kirk might not report to him, but she couldn't imagine there was much at Jones Inc. of which he wasn't aware or hadn't orchestrated.

His gaze not meeting hers, Joseph shook his head.

"Well, I guess you're a little overdressed to talk to an employee," she remarked, trying to ignore how his muscular body filled out the black tuxedo he wore with no bow tie, just the white pleated shirt sharply contrasting his dark hair and honey-toned skin. "If you want to see Thora, I think she's out, too, at some political fund-raiser or benefit—"

"Yeah, I escorted her," he said.

"Oh, you just brought her home?" And decided to look in on Elena after? She couldn't imagine why…unless he was accepting the challenge she'd unwittingly presented herself as at their last encounter.

Excitement quickened her pulse and shortened her breath as an image flashed through her mind. Green eyes dilated darkly with passion. A chest, dusted with black hair, rising and falling with harsh breaths. A hard body pressed tight against hers. She struggled to draw a deep breath into her suddenly constricted lungs. All she inhaled was his scent, of citrus soap and musk.

He didn't look at her as he shook his head. "No, your grandmother's still at the fund-raiser."

"So you skipped out on Thora?" She whistled under her breath, impressed despite her animosity toward him.

Dismissively he shrugged, his shoulders appearing even broader in his tux. "She has a driver."

"But if she asked you to accompany her, I'm sure she expected you to stay until she was ready to leave." Elena would much prefer he were with Thora than her. What if his late night visit brought on another dream? "Maybe you can get back before she realizes you're gone."

His lips twitched into that wicked grin as she reached for the door handle. "Trying to get rid of me, Elena?"

Unlike her grandmother who shortened her name to Elle, Joseph always called her Elena. The sound of her name in his deep voice quickened her pulse even more. She clenched her fingers into a fist, fighting her reaction to him. "Since you know Thora's still at the benefit, I'm not sure why you're here."

Under his breath he murmured, "You're not the only one…."

From the way he wouldn't meet her gaze, she had a feeling his visit had nothing to do with a challenge. "What's wrong—" She'd nearly called him Joseph but stopped herself before giving him the satisfaction.

"Does there have to be something wrong for me to come see you?" he asked, his green eyes gleaming as he finally looked at her.

Elena's heart reacted to his flirting with a sudden jump. She infused her voice with ice, something she'd learned well from her grandmother, when she replied, "Yes."

Her imperious tone didn't discourage him. His eyes only gleamed brighter. "Really? I can't stop by just to visit you?" he teased, as he stepped closer to her, invading her space with his imposing presence.

She locked her knees, so she wouldn't step back. Like Thora, he wasn't someone to whom she would ever wittingly reveal weakness. She lifted her chin and reminded him, "I'm a married woman."

Until Kirk signed the damned papers.

"I talked to Kirk today."

She held her breath, so it wouldn't shudder out from between her suddenly parted lips. "You know I'm getting a divorce."

And he'd come right over? Why? She'd never given him any encouragement but in her dreams.

"I'm sorry, Elena," he said.

She would have doubted his sincerity, but sympathy and regret deepened his voice. "I didn't think you had much use for the institution," she mused aloud.

His lips twitched again. "Just because it's not for me doesn't mean that I don't respect it."

Maybe he would have respected his vows more than Kirk had, but then he wasn't likely to ever get married. He'd made it clear his priorities were money and power. Maybe if she kept reminding herself, she would stop having the dreams.

The lightning flashed behind her eyelids, signaling the beginning of a vision. She fought hard to suppress it, squeezing her eyes shut, afraid that it might be the one where she was naked, lying in his arms. She didn't understand that dream; it wasn't that she subconsciously wanted him. She couldn't, not when she didn't respect or trust him. After Kirk's infidelity, she wasn't likely to trust *any* man, ever again.

"Elena, are you okay?"

Eyes still closed, she nodded. "Yeah, yeah, I'm fine."

This wasn't one of those brief flashes where images flitted through her mind. This was deeper, the paralyzing grip of a complete vision. She rallied her strength, fighting against it. She concentrated instead on his voice, which seemed to come at her from a distance.

"Divorce can be tough, so I've heard. If you need anything…"

Surprised by his offer, she opened her eyes. Then

pride lifted her chin and once again permeated her words with ice. "I don't need *your* help."

He didn't grin this time, his eyes darkening as if she'd offended or hurt him. But she knew better. *She* couldn't hurt him. She could only be hurt by *him*.

"If you ever do need my help," he continued, as if she hadn't rudely thrown his offer back in his face, "I'm here for you, Elena."

She was almost as afraid of his closeness as she was her visions, but if he were sincere, maybe she could use his help. He might be able to aid in the search for her baby sister. He'd grown up on the streets. If Elena had interpreted her visions of Irina correctly, her sister was living on the streets. He might be able to help Elena find her.

Before she could open her mouth to ask him, the lightning flashed again inside her head, too bright and blinding to be suppressed. Even though she kept her eyes wide open, the images began to play out in her mind like the reel of an old home movie. This wasn't her and Joseph tangled up in each other's arms. This was worse. Pain pierced her temples as the lightning brightened, illuminating the person in her vision.

Stacia cowered in a confined place, in the dark. Her little body shaking in her pajamas, the ones Elena had helped her into just a little while ago, the pink ones with the fluffy white sheep, each of them wearing a number, dancing on them. She'd taught Stacia to recognize numbers by pointing to them on those pajamas.

Where was her baby? Elena had to know. She closed her eyes, trying to focus on the vision, but the shadows thickened, obscuring everything but Stacia, lying alone in that tight, dark place but for her teddy bear, the fluffy white one that was so hard to keep clean Elena had to sneak it into the washing machine when Stacia was sleeping. Why was her baby alone in the dark? Stacia was terrified of the dark.

Elena hadn't had a dream or vision of Stacia in so long, not since the one of her being born. Why now? Was Stacia in danger?

The pain intensified, hammering at Elena's temples with such force that her knees weakened. As she swayed on her feet, strong hands closed over her shoulders, steadying her. But she couldn't feel the touch, nor could she hear anything for the roar of fear in her ears, rushing through her pulsing veins.

Inside her head, in the vision, hands came out of the shadows, big hands reaching for Stacia, closing around her thin arms, dragging her out of her hiding place.

The muscles in Elena's stomach clenched. Why had Stacia been hiding? Where was Stacia? Who was reaching for her?

Stacia's blue eyes widened with fear, and she twisted in the grasp of the unknown man. But the hands only tightened, squeezing her delicate little arms until her mouth opened in a cry of pain.

"No!" Elena yelled, overcome with the need to protect her child.

The hands on Elena's shoulders gripped harder, shaking her. "What the hell's going on? What's wrong?" Joseph shouted his questions, as if he'd asked before and been ignored. Undoubtedly he wasn't used to being ignored.

Elena blinked open her eyes and stared up into his face, his brow furrowed in confusion. Choked with fear, all she could do was whisper, "Stacia…"

"She's upstairs, right? Asleep?" he asked, his concern vibrating in his voice.

Elena drew in a deep breath, trying to calm herself. Her visions were of the *future,* not the present. And they didn't always come true. If they did, Ariel wouldn't still be alive. Stacia was fine. Her pulse leapt as she added her next thought. Now.

"I put her to bed," she told Joseph and reminded herself. "She was in bed."

"Then she's *still* in bed," Joseph assured her, as he studied her intently.

No one had ever witnessed Elena having a vision before. She'd been careful to conceal them while awake, even if she'd had to rush from a room during the middle of a conversation, and if a dream had interrupted her sleep, she'd insisted it was just a dream.

"Everything's fine," Joseph insisted, so eerily calm and reassuring that he unsettled her as much as the vision. Nobody had ever offered her such solid support.

Her breath hitched, burning in her lungs as she held it. "I have to check on her," she said, heading for the staircase on the other side of the living room. For peace of mind, she needed to assure herself Stacia was safely in her bed. Climbing in haste, Elena missed a step. Again the big hand closed over her shoulder, guiding her, as Joseph ascended the stairs behind her.

"Careful," he said.

She had been. Since realizing someone had resurrected the witch hunt, she'd hardly taken Stacia off the estate. But the killer wouldn't go after her daughter. Stacia wasn't a witch. She didn't have any special abilities.

Elena swallowed hard as she remembered Stacia's nightmares. And once at the park, Stacia had claimed to see a child Elena couldn't see. She'd thought then that her creative little girl had made up an imaginary friend. But what if the invisible child had been a ghost…

No. Elena could not think of her daughter as cursed. She turned her head, glancing over her shoulder at Joseph. "You don't need to come with me."

But he stayed close as she walked down the hall toward her daughter's room. "Elena, what—what the hell happened down there? You completely spaced out, like you were staring at something inside your head. And now you're all shook up. What the hell are you—"

"An overprotective mother." And she would keep her sweet daughter safe inside the wrought iron-gates of the estate, tucked up in her little bed with the Strawberry Shortcake lamp dispelling the shadows in her room. Her daughter wouldn't *ever* be left alone in the dark.

Unsettled by Joseph's probing questions, Elena banged her shoulder against the doorjamb as she walked into Stacia's room. But no one stirred sleepily, awakened by the noise. The covers were already pulled back, the bed empty. Her baby was gone.

Elena reached out, clutching Joseph's arm as he stood in the doorway behind her. "Joseph, where is she?"

Before he could say anything, she released him and ran to the bathroom adjacent to Stacia's room.

The bulb of the night-light glowed in the empty space. "She's not here!"

"I'll check with Mrs. Chapin," Joseph said, referring to the housekeeper as he headed back into the hall.

Legs weak, Elena dropped onto Stacia's mussed-up twin-sized bed. She pulled the covers aside, but no little white teddy bear was tangled in the blankets.

She hoped Joseph found her daughter with the housekeeper, but the hope was faint as fear of her vision tugged at her. The image rolled through her mind again, of her daughter cowering alone in the dark. The dingy white bear her only company… until hands reached for her.

She wrapped her arms around herself, unable to dispel the cold that chilled her deep inside. For the first time since she'd given birth to her, Elena didn't know where her daughter was.

Chapter 4

Guilt twisted Joseph's gut. He'd suspected something like this was going to happen but still he'd done nothing to stop it, to prevent her pain. He leaned against the doorjamb, watching Elena as she sat on her daughter's bed, her arms wrapped tightly around herself as if they were all that held her together.

"Elena," he called to her, regret eating at him that he'd left her alone so long. Had she gone to that place again, inside her head? He edged away from the door, stepping deeper into the room, getting closer to her even though he knew he shouldn't, that he didn't have the right. Even if she wasn't still a married woman, she was out of his league.

"She isn't here," Elena said without looking up from her daughter's rumpled sheets.

He drew in a deep breath. "No, she isn't."

"How did he get her?" she asked, her voice soft, lost. She rose from the bed and walked toward him. "After I tucked her in, I was in the living room, right between the door and the stairs. How—"

He pressed a finger against her lips, stemming her self-recrimination. "There's a doorway on this floor, at the end of the hall, that opens to the main house."

"But that door's always locked—"

He shook his head. "Not tonight."

Her breath shuddered out, soft against his finger. "I never thought he'd take her."

"Elena," he said, reaching for her trembling body. She didn't recoil like she usually did from his touch. As his arms closed around her, she clutched at his shirt, knotting the pleats in her fingers.

Her voice rose with a note of hysteria. "She's gone! He has her—"

"Elena, he's not going to hurt her—"

"He's going to kill her!" she cried as she stared up at him, her light blue eyes wild with fear.

Shocked by her outburst, his arms tightened around her, as if he had to hold her together now. "Elena, what the hell are you talking about? He's her father—"

"What?" she asked, pulling back to stare up at him, those eerie blue eyes wide. "Kirk took Stacia?"

He nodded. "Mrs. Chapin said he was here earlier, in the main house."

"I didn't know he was back from his last trip. And as for being in the main house, he's been staying there for a while," Elena admitted.

So divorce hadn't been an impulsive decision for her. She and Kirk had already been separated. Joseph refused to analyze why that knowledge lifted something in his chest; he doubted it was his heart, like his soul, he'd lost that a long time ago. But hell, he didn't care; he didn't need what he never intended to use. He drew an envelope from the inside pocket of his tuxedo and handed it to Elena. "He left this note with Mrs. Chapin."

Elena fumbled the envelope open and drew out the folded paper. Her brow furrowed as she read, but when she finished and lifted her gaze to Joseph's, her blue eyes were clear, less troubled than before, as if she were relieved. "Yes, Kirk has her," she confirmed.

The pressure on Joseph's chest eased a bit,

but he still had a lot of questions about Elena's reactions. Something else was going on here besides a messy divorce. *It's not any of your business, Joe.* He had a feeling that it wouldn't matter how many times he told himself that, he'd still want to know what was really going on with Elena.

"So what did Kirk say?" Joseph asked, wishing he'd put aside his sudden attack of scruples and had read the letter her husband had left for her.

Elena tucked the paper back inside the envelope, then clutched it tight in her hand. "You should get back to the benefit before Thora notices you're missing."

"Forget Thora," he said, realizing he didn't care about the woman who'd made him rich. "I'm worried about *you*."

Elena lifted her chin. "Don't. Worry about yourself. When Thora—"

"I don't give a damn about Thora!" he shouted, frustrated that Elena wouldn't accept his concern, that she wouldn't share hers with him. But guilt gnawed at him again. If he'd felt that way earlier, when Thora had threatened to fire him if he didn't carry out her orders, Elena might know where her daughter was.

"You're not afraid of her," Elena mused, a bit of awe in her voice.

"Fear is something I stopped feeling a long time ago." If he hadn't, he wouldn't have survived growing up on the streets. Alone. Hungry. Desperate. He hadn't had room for fear.

But because he still remembered being hungry and desperate, he hadn't wanted to give up his job. Elena had asked him the other day what Thora held over him; it was that. If he left Jones Inc., she'd make sure he'd never hold another powerful position. She might even send him to jail, if she wanted to risk going there herself. *She* might have been crazy enough to risk it, but Joseph wasn't. Growing up, he'd spent a little time in jail. Confined. Powerless. He didn't want to go back.

Elena sighed and made another surprising admission. "Sometimes fear is *all* I feel."

"Elena, he's not going to hurt her—"

"I know."

"But you said—"

She shook her head. "I wasn't thinking straight earlier. I was just reacting to my little girl being gone. Stacia has never spent a night away from me. I just want her home."

"So call Kirk."

She sighed again. "He's not going to bring her back just because I tell him to."

"Then *I'll* tell him." With his fists once he found

the weasel. When he'd suspected Kirk might pull something stupid, he'd warned her husband that if he hurt Elena, Joseph would kill him.

Instead of being impressed with his offer, she laughed. "Kirk is running because he's scared. Scaring him more is not going to bring him back here."

Confusion drew Joseph's brows together. "I thought he just wanted money." He gestured toward the envelope in her hand, containing what he'd figured was basically a ransom note; now he wondered.

"What's he scared of?" Joseph's threat? God, he hoped that wasn't why the bastard had taken off with her daughter.

She surprised him more when she calmly stated, "Me."

He drew in a quick breath. "Elena, what aren't you telling me?"

She shook her head, refusing to reveal any more of her secrets. "It's better if you don't know."

"Who's it better for? You or me?" he wondered aloud.

She studied him a moment, gnawing at her lower lip. Then she softly replied, "Both of us."

"When Thora first made me CEO, I started visiting your dad. He talked so much about you that I thought I knew everything. Then you tell me the other day about being poor. And now…" The way she'd acted, as if hypnotized into a trance.

"I'm a distraught mother."

"You'll get Stacia back."

"I have to," she muttered, "before it's too late…."

"Elena, I want to help you." He didn't know why, hadn't even been able to explain to himself why he'd left the fund-raiser to check on her. *Helping* people was not his thing. No one had ever helped him. He'd taken care of himself. But he liked her little kid. Stacia was a sweetheart. And despite *her* never being all that sweet to him, he liked Elena, too. Maybe because she wasn't all that sweet to him. The challenge thing again? Or did it go deeper?

"Then leave me *alone,*" she said, all prickly pride again, as her eyes and voice got icy.

Maybe she was high-society now, but somewhere inside Elena lurked a street fighter like him, determined to take care of herself. But she wasn't selfish like him; she'd taken care of her father and daughter, too. He didn't know which attracted him more, her compassion or her stubborn self-reliance. "Elena…"

"Go back to Thora," she advised him. "You don't want to risk losing your job. I know how important it is to you."

Getting less important with every contact he

had with Elena. He should have refused to do Thora's bidding; he'd told her no before, on other things. But she'd only threatened to fire him this once…when it had to do with Elena.

He needed to leave her alone, just like she wanted. He wrestled into submission his desire to know what was really going on. She wanted him gone, and he needed to heed his instincts, the ones that warned him against getting involved any deeper with her. She was the kind of woman who needed more than a man like him could give. He'd vowed long enough to never be anyone's husband or father.

"I'll leave you alone for now."

That was all he could promise either of them.

"I called the police," Elena said, but her sister didn't lift her gaze from reading the letter Kirk had left when he'd taken Stacia. "They told me to call a lawyer."

"Did you?" Ariel asked.

Elena nodded although she'd done more than call. The lawyer had been her first stop before coming here, to the penthouse Ariel shared with her fiancé, David. Elena paced over to the windows, which stretched from marble floor to vaulted plaster ceiling. Several stories below her the lights of Barrett sparkled against the black

backdrop of night. The lawyer had complained
that she'd stopped by too late.

Her hands fisted as anger and frustration gripped
her. And fear. She worried she'd be too late to protect
her daughter, to stop the hands from reaching for her.
"*My* lawyer agreed with Kirk. If we go to court, I
stand a good chance of losing Stacia."

Ariel blew out a ragged breath. "I didn't even
know you were getting divorced."

"I thought I could handle it by myself. Then
Kirk pulled this…"

Ariel joined Elena at the windows, the letter
crumpled in her trembling hand. "You don't have
to handle everything by yourself anymore."

Having someone to turn to was a new sensation
for Elena; she'd always had to be the strong one,
for her dad, for Kirk, for Stacia.

"I wasn't sure I should come here," she admitted.

"Why?"

"Because you know now that I'm a McGregor."

"You're my sister," Ariel said. "Of course I'm
going to help you."

She wasn't the only one who'd offered; Joseph
wanted to help, too. Why? He couldn't care about
her; she'd never given him any reason to. What did
he think was in it for him if he helped? The memory
of a vision played through her mind, naked limbs
entangled, lips melded, bodies joined…

"Elena," her sister called to her. "I'm going to wake up David. I'd call Ty, too." He was David's best friend, a cop, though suspended from the police force. His first favor for Ariel had cost him his job when the suspect he'd tried to arrest for abusing one of Ariel's students had died; his second had almost cost him his life on the floor of the church where Ariel and David had nearly died as well. There was nothing Ty wouldn't do for Elena's sister. "But he's working hard on trying to track down Irina and the killer. He checks in, but he's hard to get a hold of."

"Don't take him away from his search." If Ty found the killer first, Stacia would be safe. And Irina, too.

"I agree. Ty needs to stay focused on finding the killer. And Irina. But don't worry," Ariel assured her, "between you, me and David, we'll find Stacia."

Her daughter wasn't all that was missing. Before she'd left the house, Elena had searched for her pewter star. She'd wanted to use its warmth and presence for reassurance. For the security she'd never really known. But the charm was gone. Kirk, having seen her reach for it after nightmares, must have realized how important it was to her, so he'd taken it, too.

As Ariel moved to step around her, Elena caught her hand. "When he took Stacia, he took something else, too."

She lowered her chin, unable to meet her sister's questioning gaze. She knew how much faith Ariel had in the charms, that she believed reuniting them was the only way to stop the witch hunt. By letting the star out of her sight, by letting it get stolen, she'd let down her sister. Again.

"So tell me—what did he take?" Ariel prodded.

"The charm."

Her sister's breath audibly caught, then she released it in a shaky sigh. "That's okay. That's good. It's with Stacia. It'll keep her safe."

Tears burned Elena's eyes, but she blinked them away. "I had a vision of her," she shared, "before I realized she was gone."

Ariel's hand gripped hers, offering a reassuring squeeze. "What did you see?"

"My daughter, hiding in the dark. She hates the dark." She swallowed hard, forcing down the fear that threatened to overwhelm her.

"Elena, I'm so sorry…."

"*He* finds her, Ariel. He pulls her out of her hiding place. And he hurts her." She squeezed her eyes shut, but she couldn't force the image from her mind, the vision of those big hands tightening around Stacia's arms until she cried out in pain.

Ariel pulled her into a hug. "No, he won't. We'll find her first."

Elena borrowed some of her sister's optimism

and nodded. "You're right. We will find her first. Go ahead, wake David."

In finding Stacia, they had not a moment to lose. Elena never knew how much time would pass before her vision would become reality.

As Ariel released her, Elena took back the letter, but she didn't need to reread it; she'd already memorized the hateful words. *I know the truth. You're crazy, unfit to be a wife and most certainly unfit to be a mother.*

Kirk had dug up her past, the psychiatric visits, the anti-hallucinatory drugs. But his last line had been the worst. *Stacia will be better off with me.*

Was he right? With a killer stalking her mother and aunts, maybe Stacia was safer with her father. For the first time in twenty years, Elena understood her mother a little. Myra had made a difficult decision to protect her daughters by giving them up. Elena hadn't always believed it was the right decision, but now she could respect how hard it had been for Myra to make. Could Elena do the same? Could she leave her daughter with Kirk and never see her again?

But she couldn't forget her vision. Who was Stacia with when she was hiding? Kirk or *her?*

A tear trickled from the corner of her eye. She reached up to dash it away with the back of her hand, accepting she wasn't as strong as her mother had been. *She* couldn't let Stacia go. She had to be with her daughter. *She* had to be the one to keep her safe.

"Damn him!" she yelled, slamming her fist against the window. The glass shuddered beneath her hand, as if threatening to crack. Like she'd cracked with, of all people, Joseph Dolce.

Great, Elena, show your weakness with the strongest person you know. She knew that from what she'd heard about him, how he'd grown up on the streets and still made a success of himself. But she hadn't turned down his offer to help out of pride, or regret over breaking down in front of him. Even though she'd actually known Joseph longer than she'd known her sister, as an adult, she still didn't know him well enough to trust him, not to find her daughter. Her dreams, of the two of them together, didn't count. They were just dreams.

Like the one that had awakened Stacia a few nights before. She'd been hiding because something bad had happened to her father. Was that where she was in Elena's vision, hiding from whoever was hurting Kirk? Elena didn't think those were Kirk's arms reaching for her. Someone else found her daughter.

Although the night remained black and still, lightning flashed through Elena's mind, blinding her. She leaned her forehead against the cool glass of the window and closed her eyes. The jagged beam chased the shadows from her head, leaving only vivid color.

Red. Flowing in rivulets across a threadbare carpet, pooling beneath the crumpled body of a woman. Hair once long and blond turned dark and sticky with blood.

Was that *Elena's* hair? Was *she* bleeding to death? The bloody hair lay across the face, hiding it from her inner gaze. She could only follow those trails of blood…to another body, lying face up on the carpet. His eyes open with surprise and fear, Kirk lay dead on the floor. Neon lights from a motel sign flashed across the skin of his chest, bare but for the blood covering it.

So much blood.

Is this what Stacia would see? Her father, maybe her mother, killed? Or was that why she was hiding in the dark, she'd chosen an old fear over a new one?

The first light of dawn streaked through the blinds, painting gold stripes across the bed where Stacia lay. She was supposed to be sleeping, but she hadn't been able to do that since Daddy had brought her here. She wasn't tired even though she felt like she had sand in her eyes. She blinked hard, but her lids were so heavy she could actually catch glimpses of the fringe of the curly lashes on the rims of them.

She didn't want to sleep in this hard bed. She wanted to be back home, in her room, with Mommy singing her a lullaby or reading her a story that Stacia could really read herself.

"Mommy…" she murmured, reaching out, but her hands closed around plush velour and a soft, stuffed body. Teddy.

Daddy had given her Teddy years ago, when she was a baby. Mommy had called him im-prack-able because Teddy's fur was white and probably wouldn't stay that way. It wasn't now. He'd fallen in the parking lot, his fur matted with some black splotches and smelling like a gas station.

Mommy would have cleaned him up before allowing him in bed, but Daddy hadn't even noticed. He was too busy looking over his shoulder and hurrying around, him and his friend. The lady tried to be nice, talking soft and sweet to Stacia, but she wasn't Mommy.

Stacia wanted Mommy.

The door creaked open, not the one to the outside cement hallway thing, but the one to the other room where Daddy and his friend had slept last night. Stacia closed her eyes. She and Daddy would both be happier if he thought she was sleeping. Then she wouldn't have to see that look on his face, that one like he'd watched a scary movie.

He hadn't though. She was the one who'd had the scary movie playing inside her head, but when she told him about it, he got scared, too. As scared as she was. That was why he'd taken her away from home, he'd said, to keep her safe.

"But what about Mommy?" she'd asked.

"Mommy wasn't in your dream. She's safe. You and me are the ones that aren't," he'd reminded her.

Not that she ever wanted to remember what she'd seen. The bad man in his brown robe. The blood. All kinds of blood. On Daddy. His friend.

Stacia snuggled deeper in the blankets, but they were cold and scratchy. Daddy had left her favorite soft one in the car, but she didn't want to ask him to get it. He was probably too scared to go outside, like Stacia was too scared to go to sleep. Because she didn't want to dream again.

She wished she'd never told Daddy, then he wouldn't be scared. And she'd be home in her own bed and Mommy would be with her.

Mommy was *always* with her.

She waited until the door creaked closed again, then she pushed off the blankets and climbed out of bed. Her Strawberry Shortcake backpack lay on the floor. Daddy had packed some of her clothes and her toothbrush. Stacia had packed something far more important. She unzipped a small pocket at the front and reached inside, pulling out a little star.

The metal was warm against her skin, so warm that Stacia pressed it against her cheek. Some flowery scent mixed with something a little sharper drifted to her nose, reminding her of Mommy. She hoped Mommy wouldn't be mad that she'd taken it. But she'd wanted something of Mommy's to keep with her, something to keep Mommy close to her.

Stacia squeezed her eyes shut and tried hard to concentrate. Sometimes when she did that, she could tell what Mommy was thinking. But she couldn't hear any of *her* thoughts now, only her own. A tear slipped through her lashes and streaked down her cheek. She rubbed it away with the little metal star.

The charm, and the scent clinging to it, also reminded her of Grandma. Not the blond-haired lady who made her call her Grandmother and sit like a doll on those fussy little chairs in her parlor, but the other lady, the one who looked like a gypsy from one of Stacia's books. With black curly hair and big dark eyes.

Stacia had only been seeing her for a little while, but she was the only one who could. Except for Aunt Ariel. Mommy couldn't see Grandma Myra.

Stacia wished that one of them were with her now, so she wasn't all alone and so scared that the bad man was going to come for her like he did in her dream.

Chapter 5

A major shareholder in Jones Inc. since her father's death, Elena didn't need an appointment to see Joseph. The receptionist led her straight back to his office. Maybe waiting would have been better; she might have come to her senses and changed her mind about seeking his help. But after staying awake all night going over her visions and everything she knew about Kirk with Ariel and her fiancé, Elena had few senses left. And few options.

To find Stacia before the killer, she could leave no stone unturned, even the one under which she used to think Joseph lived. But after last night, after the concern he'd showed her, she had trouble hanging onto her formerly low opinion of him.

The receptionist opened the door to his inner sanctum. Two walls of windows met in a corner; the two inside walls were mahogany panels trimmed in brass. Despite the dark wood, all the windows, bare of blinds or curtains, bathed the room with bright light. The classy office befitted a CEO of a major corporation. She could imagine how far from the streets, in more than elevation, it must seem to a man who'd grown up like he had.

Joseph stood and walked around his massive, mahogany desk, just as elegant in a dark suit as he was last night in his tux. His shirt, a light green, brought out the vibrant color of eyes that were soft with concern and regret. "He didn't bring her back," he gleaned from her expression.

She'd stopped at the house to check, but Stacia's room remained eerily empty without the little girl's sweet presence. She blinked back tears, of fear and frustration and exhaustion, and shook her head. "That's why I'm here."

His green eyes flickered. "You want *my* help? When I offered last night, you weren't interested."

Drawing on the strength of her pride, she lifted her chin. "I'm not sure I should trust you, Joseph."

The corners of his lips lifted, a shadow of his

usual wicked grin. "At least you've finally started using my first name."

She had. Last night. She'd had an excuse to use it then, when the vision had unhinged her. But today...today she couldn't go back to calling him Mr. Dolce. The words stuck in her throat. "*Should* I trust you, Joseph?"

He didn't answer her question with his response. "I'll help you find Stacia. She's a neat little kid. She should be with her mother. Kirk doesn't deserve her."

Kirk couldn't protect her. He was too weak and soon he might be dead. "You know my daughter?"

His lips lifted again in a full smile. "Every time I stop by the house, she and I visit for a while. She shows me some toy, or how she jumps rope." He shook his head. "I wasn't supposed to tell you she does that in the house. It's our little secret."

Joseph Dolce and her daughter shared secrets? She blinked hard, clearing her eyes.

"You keep Stacia's secrets. And Thora's." She had no doubt the old woman had many. "What about Kirk's? Did you know about his affair?"

Even though Kirk didn't report directly to Joseph, she doubted there was much of which he wasn't aware. His nod confirmed her suspicions. "So that's why you filed," he said.

"His infidelity is just one of the reasons."

Because if she counted her dreams, Kirk wasn't the only one who'd cheated on their marriage.

"He doesn't deserve *you* either, Elena."

She refused to be swayed by his compliment. Except in her dreams, she was immune to his charm. "You should have told *me*."

He shrugged. "I wasn't sure you wanted to know. And I didn't think you'd believe me."

She probably wouldn't have, if she hadn't seen Kirk and the woman in her head, wrapped up in each other's arms. "So who is she?"

His brow furrowed. "Elena—"

"I don't care about their affair." She didn't want to, in a jealous fit, track down the woman. She had no time for that. "My daughter might be with her," she pointed out. "Who is she?"

"Felicia Hanover. She works in Kirk's department."

"Is she here today?"

He shook his head. "She didn't show up for work."

"Give me her address."

"I checked her place last night," he said, "and again this morning before I came into work. I caught her landlord. He said she left yesterday… with suitcases."

Elena's breath shuddered out. "So they planned this."

Joseph nodded. "Didn't he say as much in the letter he left you?"

"You really didn't read it." Although he hadn't acted as if he had, she'd had her suspicions that he'd violated her privacy. Since he hadn't, maybe she could trust him.

A light flashed inside her mind as images began to play. Her and Joseph, entwined, on his couch. She lay beneath him, his long, hard body pressing her into the leather until he eased up. His hands reached for her blouse, his big fingers fumbling with the little mother-of-pearl buttons before parting the yellow silk. His breath shuddered out, warm against her face, before his lips touched hers.

"You're so beautiful," he murmured against her mouth.

She'd been told that before; his compliment shouldn't have affected her. But her heart shifted, her pulse quickening. His lips brushed across hers in soft, teasing kisses.

Then his hand settled over her breast, over the satin cup of her lemon-yellow bra. "You're so beautiful here," he said. "Inside."

No one had complimented her heart before. She opened her mouth, inviting him to deepen the kiss. But still he teased, lapping at her lower lip with his tongue, then nibbling with his teeth, before finally giving her the kiss she wanted. Hot and possessive, his mouth pressed against hers, his tongue sweeping inside, filling her.

Her heart raced beneath the palm of his hand as his fingers caressed the mound that spilled over the top of the bra. "Joseph, more," she pleaded against his mouth as she clawed at the knot of his tie, pulling it free of the collar of his green shirt.

He'd already discarded his suit jacket, which lay on the floor beside the couch, along with her high-heeled pumps. She reached now for his buttons, her nails scraping his skin as she pulled his shirt open. He groaned, and his erection strained against his pants and pressed hard against her hip. "Elena…"

She lifted her hips, rubbing her pelvis against him.

His hands slid down her body, clasping her waist to hold her still. "I want to take my time with you," he said, his voice low with the sensual threat.

Heat pooled between her legs as her passion burned higher. She reached for his belt. "I want you now," she insisted, using the imperious tone she'd learned so well.

He chuckled, then flashed his wicked grin, as he shifted his hips away from her so that she couldn't unbuckle his belt.

"I don't take orders well," he warned her. Then

he unclasped her bra, pushing aside the satin cups to free her breasts. Instead of touching them, he stared, his hot gaze an erotic caress.

Her skin flushed, and her nipples hardened, lifting up and begging for his touch. Elena drew her bottom lip between her teeth, biting the soft flesh, as she arched her back.

"You're bad," Joseph admonished her. "Very, very bad." Then he dipped his head, caressing her skin with his breath before touching his lips to her. His mouth trailed moist kisses around the curve of her breasts.

Elena shifted against the leather as her frustration built. She wanted more. She needed more. "Joseph…"

A big hand settled over her shoulder, pulling Elena from the erotic vision. She shuddered with frustration, as heat and passion flushed her face and her body. She wrapped her arms around herself, so she wouldn't reach for him and finish what had begun in her dream.

Only a dream. It wasn't real. None of it was real. But the touch of his hand on her shoulder was, his palm leaving an imprint in the yellow silk of her blouse and on her skin beneath. She'd never been so aware of him…so desperate with wanting. She drew in a shaky breath, wrestling with the last, erotic aftershocks of her vision.

"There you go again," he accused, his deep voice dousing the flames of desire the vision had fanned to life. Nothing soft and loverlike about him now, he was his usual intimidating self. "What the hell is happening to you? Where do you go inside yourself?"

She shook her head, her hair sticking to the perspiration glistening on her face as the blond tresses tumbled around her shoulders. She fought an internal battle between her reluctance to share her secret with him and her desperation for his help in finding Stacia. He had resources she didn't, and as he'd proved with having already gone to Kirk's mistress's apartment, he knew things she, Ariel and David didn't.

Would he think her crazy if she told him about the visions? But how else could she explain the urgency to find Stacia before the killer did…unless she told him everything?

"Elena?" His deep voice vibrated with concern.

She rubbed her hands over her face, pushing back her hair. "This is going to sound incredible. You're probably not going to believe me, but I'm telling you the truth."

However, the words stuck in her throat. She'd kept her secret for a long time, even from herself. She'd spent the past twenty years denying who and what she was; admitting it now wasn't easy. She paced around the room, stopping near the door, tempted to leave with her secret kept. But then an image flashed through her mind, Stacia cowering in the dark, those big hands reaching for her, squeezing her little arms until she cried out in pain. Elena flinched as her daughter's pain and fear became hers.

Joseph's hand cupped her chin, tipping it up, so she had to meet his concerned gaze. "Tell me," he prompted. "This isn't just a custody battle. I saw your face last night. You looked like you do now. Scared out of your mind."

He was right about that. She was scared. And she was probably out of her mind to confide in him.

"What's going on, Elena?"

He'd never assured her that she could trust him, but he wasn't the one she really needed to trust. She had to believe in herself first, before she could expect anyone else to do the same.

"I have two sisters," she began, in a rush.

His brow furrowed with confusion. "Your dad told me he had only you."

"He wasn't their father." She sighed. "I don't know who their fathers are. Probably neither did my mother."

"Tell me about her."

"She was a gypsy."

"A real one?" he asked, his lips tipping into a slight grin. "Living that vagabond lifestyle on the road?"

"On the run," she corrected him. "From a three-hundred-and-fifty-year-old vendetta." She blew out a breath, then continued, "That was when the McGregors swore vengeance on all the descendents of Myra Durikken, my mother's ancestor, who was believed to be a witch and subsequently burned at the stake. She had a vision of her fate and sent her daughter away before she could be killed, too. My sister Ariel and I like to believe that's why *our* mother gave us up twenty years ago, that she was protecting us, too."

If Elena hadn't had the vision of Kirk's murder, she might have done the same with Stacia, given her up for her protection. But her sacrifice wouldn't save Stacia; the only thing that would was finding her before the killer did.

"I don't understand," he said, his fingers still on her face, almost absently stroking her skin. "What does any of this have to do with Stacia and Kirk?"

Images flashed through her mind. The black-haired woman caught in the flames. Another woman being hanged. Another crushed to death. "The witch hunt has begun again, Joseph. My mother and her sisters were recently murdered."

"God, Elena, I'm sorry…."

"Me, too. I never got to see her again... except..."

"Except what?" he prompted her again, his green eyes darkening as he narrowed them.

The images rolled through her head again. The gruesome murders. The man in the shadows, concealed by the dark brown robe. A chill chased down her spine, raising goose bumps on her skin. He was out there, waiting to kill them.

"I saw her in a vision. I'm cursed, Joseph. Like Myra Durikken and my mother, Myra Cooper, I have visions. I *saw* my mother burned at the stake just like her ancestor. I *saw* one of my aunts hanged and the other crushed to death."

His hand fell away from her face, and he stepped back. Even though he'd denied he would think it of her, she could tell he wondered...was she crazy?

"If you don't believe *me*," she said, hating that her voice rose with defensiveness, hating that she cared that he didn't believe her, "talk to David Koster."

"The computer mogul?" His brow creased again. "What does he have to do with any of this?"

Elena lifted her chin, refusing to be ashamed any longer of who she was. She wasn't twelve years old anymore and easily manipulated or intimidated. "David is engaged to my sister. He knows everything."

And he believed Ariel. But then he loved her. Elena wasn't sure Joseph even liked her. Desired maybe, when he'd thought her one of those fancy women his wealth and power usually attracted. But now he knew the truth, whether or not he accepted it.

"I wish you'd tell *me* everything," he said, then drew in a breath, as if trying to collect his thoughts. "You didn't answer my earlier question. What does this 'witch hunt' have to do with Stacia and Kirk?"

"I had a vision last night, that Stacia was somewhere in the dark, alone and hiding."

The creases smoothed out as understanding glimmered. "That's why you went tearing upstairs to check on her."

She nodded. "Then later I had another one, of Kirk dying." And maybe she died with him. "Is Felicia Hanover blond?"

Joseph shrugged. "She's lower level. I've only seen her a couple of times. I don't remember her hair color. Maybe brown. Maybe dark blond."

Fear rose, choking Elena. Maybe *she* herself was the one who died with Kirk. Who would save Stacia then? For the first time in her life, she had to rely on others, on her sister and her fiancé. And Joseph?

"I have to find Stacia before the killer does," she

said, her voice rising with the hysteria she'd fought so hard to subdue. "David's running Kirk's credit cards, but he hasn't used them yet. David also has his friend, a suspended cop, asking his former colleagues to keep an eye out for Kirk's car." Or he would when Ty checked in.

She didn't want to ask Ty to do anything more. All his efforts were concentrated on the search for Irina, so the killer wouldn't find her before they did. As an image of the black-haired woman, bound to the stake, flashed through her mind, Elena shuddered. Nobody would be safe until the killer was caught. And that was where the other half of Ty's concentration was centered, on finding the killer.

"Since you've been honest with me, I have to be honest with you, Elena." Joseph sighed and rubbed his hand over his jaw. "I saw Kirk yesterday, before he took off. I gave him a lot of money. He might have bought a different car, and he probably won't need to use his credit cards for a while."

What little hope she'd had in David's ability to track down Kirk evaporated. Only dread filled her now. She'd trusted the wrong man to help her. "You paid him to take off with Stacia?"

"No. That wasn't the intention." But from his tone, he'd obviously realized it was a possibility, which explained the reason for his visit last night. "At least I don't think that's what Thora intended."

Her grandmother had betrayed her before, but still the old woman's action struck Elena like a blow. How could Thora hate her so much? Just because she was Myra's daughter?

"So *she* told you to give Kirk the money." Her heart clenched with the pain of yet another betrayal. "Do you think she told him to take Stacia?"

He sighed. "I don't know what to think about your grandmother."

"But yet you work for her."

"She pays me." His throat moved as he swallowed hard. "Well."

"And you do her dirty work. So what was last night's visit about—an attack of conscience?"

"Don't make that mistake about me, Elena," he said, his voice deep with warning, as he stepped closer to her, backing her against the closed door. "I don't have a conscience."

Her breath hitched, but she refused to let him intimidate her. Or mislead her any more. She lifted her chin, unintentionally bringing her face closer to his. His green gaze studied her mouth, running over her lips, as if he'd like to devour them. Mouth dry, she slid her tongue out, and his eyes flickered with desire. She wasn't the only one having thoughts she had no business entertaining.

"Why'd you come by last night then?" she asked.

He shrugged again, drawing her attention to the breadth of his shoulders, as he admitted, "I had a feeling that he might do something stupid."

And he'd been worried about her. Despite his claim, he did have a conscience.

"He seemed desperate yesterday." Regret flickered in his green eyes. "Desperate men do crazy things."

She suspected he spoke from experience. Is that how he'd come to work for Thora? Desperation?

She turned and opened the door. But before walking away, she warned him, "Desperate women do crazy things, too."

More than desperation drove Elena as she barged into her grandmother's wing of the house. Anger held her in a fierce grip.

The floral parlor was empty but for the gardening awards, framed portraits of Elijah and the fragile, little furniture. Elena closed her fingers around the handle to the den, bracing herself for the ugly confrontation that was bound to come once she opened the door.

But the den sat dark and empty, the blinds pulled so tight at the windows that not even a sliver of light penetrated them. Only the sunshine gleaming through the parlor's tall windows spilled into the den. Elena used the sun to guide her toward Thora's desk where she flipped on the banker's lamp. Light glowed eerily through the green shade, casting strange shadows around the room.

Joseph had the seat of power in the office of CEO, but Elena knew Thora considered her seat just as powerful. She settled into the leather chair as she flipped through the files on the desk. Most of the papers looked like reports, bearing the Jones Corporation logo and Joseph's signature. He kept Thora apprised of all his decisions…until this morning. He definitely hadn't told his boss what he'd revealed to Elena.

Why would Thora pay off Kirk? She'd loved Elijah. How could she hate his daughter so much that she'd want to hurt her like this? Because she was also Myra's daughter, that was why. Myra, who'd taken Elijah away from her not just those few years he'd lived with her, but forever, because when she'd left him he'd fallen into the life of drinking and drugs that had led to his paralyzing accident. Other complications of that accident had led to his frequent bouts of pneumonia. And his death.

By that logic Elena knew that Thora also blamed Myra for Elijah's death and because Elena was Myra's daughter, she blamed her, too. Enough to start up the witch hunt again?

No. Thora was a vicious bitch, but she was no killer. Death was too quick a revenge for Thora's liking. She'd rather make her enemy suffer, as she'd made Elena suffer the past twenty years.

Elena pulled open the desk drawer. If she'd sent Kirk away with Stacia, Thora would know where they were. She had to know everything.

And so did Elena. She flipped through the papers in the drawer, trying to find something with a leasing company or a hotel address. Then she looked through cards, turning up one for a private investigator, Donovan Roarke. His business address, phone and fax numbers were embossed on the front. Undoubtedly he was the best at what he did. Thora only hired the best. Was this who she used to dig up dirt on people? Was this who had dug up the dirt about Elena's psychiatric treatments for Kirk?

No. If Kirk were acting on Thora's orders, there would have been no need to hire an investigator to tell him what the old woman already knew. She would have been the one to give him the ammunition to use against Elena, to manipulate her as Thora had for so many years.

Hand shaking, Elena pushed aside the rest of the papers and uncovered something else in the bottom of the drawer, something cold and lethal. Thora stored a gun in an unlocked desk with a child in the house?

Elena wouldn't have suspected someone as smart and controlled as her grandmother of doing something so careless…unless she felt she needed the gun readily at hand. Did she fear someone? Who?

If she had a gun in an unlocked desk, what did she have hidden away in her safe? Elena turned the chair toward the bookcase behind her. After pushing aside a few leaning, leather-bound volumes to reveal the safe, she punched in the code, her father's birthday.

This wasn't the first time Elena had searched her grandmother's office. She'd gone through the desk and safe before, when she was still a child, looking for clues to the whereabouts of her mom and sisters. She hadn't found much then, some jewelry, cash, stock certificates and an old journal. Reading the brittle pages had clued her in to her true heritage but not the location of the relatives she'd cared about. She found less now. The cash was gone, and so was the journal.

The knob rattled on the door between the parlor and the hall, so Elena slammed the safe shut and whirled back toward the desk where the detective's card stared up at her from the blotter. As the door opened, she slipped the card into the pocket of her skirt. Then she eased back in the chair, feigning nonchalance the way Thora had feigned it with her only a few short days ago.

"What are you doing in here?" her grandmother asked in that cold, imperious voice.

Elena sighed. "Just trying to figure out exactly how hateful you are."

Thora clicked her tongue against the roof of her mouth, tsking her disgust. "Talking more foolishness when you should be trying to find your daughter."

"You know she's missing because Kirk took her on *your* orders."

"I know she's missing because Mrs. Chapin told me you had Joseph looking for her. I thought you were a better mother than yours, that you'd have at least some idea of where your child is."

Anger and pain rolled through Elena, but she held it back, fighting the urge to pound her fist on the desk and scream and yell. Thora *wanted* her to lose her control. "I know you gave him money, a lot of money."

As if her legs had weakened, Thora dropped onto a chair in front of her desk. "Kirk told you that?"

She nodded, for some reason unwilling to bring Thora's wrath onto Joseph, not that he needed Elena's protection. He'd been taking care of himself for a long time.

She focused on her grandmother. "How could you…"

"I didn't pay him to take her," Thora insisted.

Elena had had enough of her grandmother's lies. "Come on—"

"I gave him money, yes, but not to take her away. I gave him money to leave. Your filing for divorce made Kirk desperate." Like Joseph had claimed. "He didn't want to give up this lifestyle. He'd grown quite used to it."

"So you gave him the money out of the goodness of your heart?" Elena voiced her disbelief.

Thora shook her head, looking every one of her seventy-three years today. "He threatened to go public."

Elena swallowed hard. "He found out about my visions, about my past."

"About your psychiatric problems," Thora said, her mouth twisting with disgust even as fear brightened her pale blue eyes. Was Elena the one she feared, the reason she kept the gun close at hand?

Until she'd married Burton Jones, Thora had been poor, like Joseph. She loved the power her position in society gave her, and the truth coming out about her granddaughter's past could threaten that position.

"Maybe Stacia is better off with her father," Thora maintained.

Elena shook her head. "I know you don't want to believe me. But someone's started up the witch hunt again. I've seen the murders I already told you about. Last night I saw *two* more."

Thora's face paled and she reached for a picture on her desk, the one of her great-granddaughter sitting on Elijah's lap. "You've seen *hers?*"

For the first time Elena realized her grandmother actually believed in her ability. "Not yet. But if I don't find her and Kirk before the killer…"

Thora lifted her gaze from the portrait, her pale eyes unfocussed. "He won't hurt her."

"Who?" Elena's heart clenched. Pulse racing, she jumped up from the chair and came around the desk to Thora. "You know who the killer is!"

The older woman shook her head. "No…"

"Thora, if you know something you have to tell me. Think about how much Stacia meant to my father. It would kill him all over again to know that she's in danger."

"She's not. She's with her father. She's safer than if she were with you. *Kirk* won't hurt her."

But Elena might?

Chapter 6

David Koster's office was opulent, with marble floor and ornate plaster ceiling. State-of-the-art computers were hooked to giant flat-panel monitors, the logo for Koster Computing flashing across them in neon letters. The door opened behind Joseph, so he turned toward the man who entered. Tall and lean with golden blond hair, Koster appeared much too young to have achieved all his success. That was one thing Joseph shared with the man; the other was the secret Elena had shared with him.

"I'm not working today, so this had better not

be about business," Koster threatened. Even his casual clothes, black silk shirt and dress pants, were expensive, more evidence of his success. "I don't have time to waste rejecting another offer from Jones In—"

"You're busy trying to find Stacia." He swallowed hard, then added, "And a killer."

Koster's dark eyes widened in surprise. "She told you?"

Joseph dragged his hand through his hair. "She told me a *lot*."

A bitter laugh slipped through Koster's lips, but no amusement lightened his dark eyes as he studied Joseph as he might some frustrating computer problem. "I'm surprised she would trust *you*."

"She doesn't." She might have if he hadn't been moved to confess giving Kirk the money, but she'd been honest with him. She believed what she'd told him; now he had to find out if *he* should believe her, too.

"She's smart," Koster said, almost as if surprised.

His attitude toward Joseph didn't offend; it was his remarks about Elena that had Joseph clenching his fists and wrestling with the urge to control his temper. He'd learned long ago that nothing good came of losing it. Control was far more powerful than rage. So he clenched his jaw and reminded the guy, "She's your fiancée's sister."

Koster shrugged. "They just reconnected after twenty years apart."

And obviously Koster wasn't the type to easily give his trust. Then again Joseph had to cut him a break if what Elena told him was true, if there was a killer on the loose.

"And she's a McGregor," Koster added.

Since the guy uttered the surname like a curse word, Joseph figured it meant something. Then he remembered the names she'd told him. The McGregors had started the witch hunt. "She's not a McGregor."

Koster nodded as if something had been asked and answered. "She may have told you a lot, but she didn't tell you *everything*."

"I know about the…" He could barely bring himself to admit it. "Witch hunt."

"A McGregor started the first one. We think a McGregor is responsible for this one, too."

Joseph shook his head, trying to get the pieces to fall into place. "I don't get it. Elena said she's the descendent of that first persecuted woman."

"Myra Durikken. She is. She's also a descendent of the man who killed her. Eli McGregor. Thora Jones named her son after him."

"Oh, my God…"

"The only McGregors left that we've been able to trace so far are Thora and—"

"Elena. You can't think…" Anger coursed through him again. "Elena would *never* hurt anyone." Unless that *anyone* harmed her child. Then she wouldn't be responsible for what she did to him. As she'd warned Joseph, she was a desperate woman.

"Elena wouldn't," Koster agreed. "But her grandmother might."

Joseph couldn't deny that, but he was compelled to point out, "She's an old woman."

"So she'd hire someone to do her dirty work." Koster's dark gaze hardened. "Isn't that why she hired you, to do her dirty work?"

Joseph blew out a ragged breath. He couldn't defend himself from all the rumors that circulated about him, just one. "I'm not a killer."

Something flickered in Koster's eyes, then he relented, "Maybe not, but I've heard you called a lot of other things."

"Man, this was a waste of my time," Joseph said, his jaw cracking.

"So why did you come here?" Koster asked. "You told my assistant it was personal, not business."

That was the only reason the man had agreed to meet with him. "I want to help find Stacia."

"And?"

He dragged in a breath. "I want to know if it's true."

"What? The witch hunt?" Koster's blond head bobbed in a nod. "Three women were brutally murdered. My fiancée was almost the fourth."

"Elena thinks Stacia might become the fourth." The look on her face, the helplessness and fear, haunted him. "I can't imagine how she must feel…."

"I can," Koster admitted with a heavy sigh.

Joseph noticed the lines of stress furrowing the guy's brow and the dark circles beneath his eyes. "You're really worried about your fiancée?"

"I was there…I had him…" A muscle jumped in Koster's cheek. Then he ran a hand along his side and grimaced. "And he got away."

"You don't know who he is."

"If I did, he'd be…"

"Dead?"

Koster shook his head. "I'm no killer, either." Again the dark eyes flickered. "But that's not all you want to know about. You wonder if the rest of it's true. Did Elena tell you about her visions?"

Joseph nodded, unable to describe what she'd told him but unable to forget what she'd said.

"Her visions are real," Koster insisted. "Ariel sees ghosts. They're gifted."

"Elena says cursed." How much of her fear was over what she saw and how much over the fact that she was able to *see?* But God, he couldn't blame her for being freaked out. He'd seen a lot of things living on the street, but he struggled to accept that what she told him was even possible.

"Elena hasn't accepted her ability yet."

She wasn't the only one.

Koster continued, "If she did…she might be able to help find her daughter."

Joseph could help, too. But just as Koster didn't trust him, he wasn't entirely sure he trusted Koster. Joseph wasn't the only one of them with a reputation for being ruthless. "How is it so easy for you to accept these supernatural abilities? You're known for being logical." Among other things.

Koster's mouth lifted in half a grin, obviously amused by what Joseph left unsaid. "I *love* Ariel. Have you ever loved anyone, Dolce?"

Joseph shook his head, but as he did, something tightened in his chest. "No."

"When you *love* someone, you automatically accept everything about her. It's what makes her who she is, who you love."

"Yeah, well…I wouldn't know about that."

Koster laughed. "You *know.* You're just not ready to admit it."

Joseph didn't like what the guy was insinuating. "Damn it—"

"So let me show you what *we* know," Koster

said, as he strode to his desk. A few strokes of his keyboard, and images sprang to life on the flat screens. Horrifying images; one dark-haired woman dangling from a rope, another's face and body bloodied and bruised beyond recognition.

"Damn it!"

"Yeah, just think, Elena saw all this first, before it ever happened. Inside her head."

Damn it!

The woman hanged. Another crushed. Elena had seen this. For the first time the full implication of what she'd told him hit Joseph. Not only was Stacia in danger from this witch-killing psychopath, so was Elena.

After spending a restless afternoon waiting by the phone for Kirk or anyone else to call her with news, Elena had come to some conclusions. She couldn't rely on Ariel and David to find her daughter, not when they couldn't find Irina or the killer. And she couldn't trust Joseph. He took his orders from Thora, who thought Stacia would be better off *without* her mother. After what Elena had told him that morning, Joseph would undoubtedly agree with Thora now.

She couldn't rely on her visions, either. She could never predict them or totally interpret them. So Elena had to hire some more help, and she wanted only the best. Maybe she was more like Thora than she cared to admit.

She reached in her pocket for the business card she'd stolen from her grandmother's desk, verified she had the right suite number, then lifted her hand to knock. But she doubted anyone was around; it was after five, the halls of the downtown Barrett building deserted. Now that she knew for certain where the office was, she would come back in the morning.

As she headed toward the bank of elevators, the door jiggled, then opened. A deep voice rumbled, "Can I help you?"

"I hope so," she murmured with relief as she turned to the man looming in the doorway. He was tall and dark, like Joseph, but his hair held glints of red instead of the almost-blue that gleamed occasionally in Joseph's. He must have been older though, for silver strands wove through the hair at his temples. "Are you Donovan Roarke, the private investigator?"

"Yes. What can I do for you?"

She'd struggled a long time with trust, mostly with trusting herself. Her instincts had inspired her to lift his card from Thora's desk. Dare she continue to trust her instincts? Dare she trust Donovan Roarke?

"I'm sorry," he said, "I don't expect you to divulge your deep, dark secrets out in the hall. Come inside."

Deep, dark secrets? Despite her silent self-as-surances, nerves danced in Elena's stomach, and she hesitated crossing the threshold into his office. "Mr. Roarke…"

He chuckled. "I'm sorry. I didn't mean to imply anything. My ex always accused me of having a sick sense of humor."

"Dry wit," she observed.

He shrugged, but his shoulders moved stiffly beneath his slightly wrinkled suit coat and his eyes briefly closed with a wince. He must have been sitting for a while, poring over files in his office or scrunched over a steering wheel for a stake-out, perhaps trying to catch a cheating spouse. Maybe if she had have hired him a while ago, she wouldn't need his services now.

"Please, come inside," he urged again.

Because he'd opened the door, she assumed he was alone. If he wasn't, the door wouldn't have been locked, and a receptionist or secretary would have met her. For a moment she wished she had lifted the gun from Thora's desk as well as the card. Then she shook off her paranoia, which was undoubtedly due to lack of sleep. She passed through the doorway in front of him.

"Excuse the mess," he said, gesturing toward the reception area piled high with boxes and files, as he led her toward his inner office which was only marginally less cluttered. "My secretary quit a while ago. I'm having a time finding a replacement. That's why I'm working late."

He lifted a stack of files from one of the chairs in front of his paneled-oak desk, dumping them onto the commercial carpet next to a box. "Have a seat."

She perched on the edge of the chair and absently remarked, "Paperwork." Not the stakeout.

He nodded grimly as he settled into the chair behind his desk. "Yup, paperwork. It's the worst."

"No." Not knowing where your child was or if she was safe, that was the worst.

"What can I help you with, Miss…?"

"Jones-Phillips." She bit her lip, then divulged, "You've done some work for my grandmother, Thora Jones."

He sighed as irritation showed in his eyes. "Well, I won't hold that against you."

"I don't think you're kidding now."

He brushed a big hand through his disheveled hair. "She's a pretty demanding client."

"Have you done much work for her?" she asked, wanting to know just how close was his association with Thora.

He shrugged, causing that wince to pinch his face again.

"Oh, I guess you can't say," she realized. "Privacy issues."

He nodded, and a lock of mahogany hair fell across his forehead. "Yeah, that was some great law the government passed." He pointed at the files on his desk and the floor around it. "All the new rules and regulations add to my paperwork, but you don't want to hear about me. What brings you here, Ms. Jones-Phillips?"

She stiffened her spine, sitting up straighter in the hard-backed chair. She wouldn't fall apart. Not again. "You can find my daughter."

He jerked, leaning across his desk. "She's missing? Have you filed a police report? Contacted the FBI?"

"Her father has her."

"Ah…" He nodded. "Nasty custody battle?"

"I just filed." Something she should have done long ago, when she'd had her first vision of his cheating. But she hadn't trusted herself then.

"The police won't get involved, not until a judge awards you custody."

But would a judge do that if Kirk made a case that her visions made her an unfit parent, if he brought up her psychiatric history?

"I can't wait until we go to court to get my daughter back," she told him.

He nodded, as a muscle twitched along his jaw. "I understand."

She studied his face, the lines fanning from his

eyes and rimming his mouth. Life appeared to have knocked him around some, too. "I believe you do."

"I've been there. Divorce is hell." He sighed, then laughed at himself. "Jeez, I don't sound bitter, huh? And it's been ten years."

"Did you have children?"

"I had a son, until the divorce. Then she took off with him."

He did understand. "She kidnapped him, too?"

"No, remarried. The judge let her take him out of the state since she had to relocate for her husband's job." That muscle twitched in his jaw again while a vein stood out at the side of his graying temple. "I see him a few weeks in the summer." He pushed his hand through his hair again. "He's a stranger to me, and I to him."

She didn't want Stacia to be a stranger. What if Kirk had taken her out of the state? Or the country? Since Joseph had given him a large sum of money, Kirk could have taken Stacia anywhere.

"Don't worry. I'll track your husband down. I'm very good at my job."

She leaned forward, fisting her hands on the edge of his desk. "I just want my daughter back." Before the killer found her.

Donovan Roarke reached across his desk and took her hands in his. A strange jolt passed between them, not anything like sexual awareness but more of recognition, as if she'd known this man before.

"I will get your daughter," he promised her.

His confidence, and his touch, should have re-assured her, but for some reason her anxiety increased, the nerves churning in her stomach as her head pounded. She pulled her hands free of his and sat back in the chair. "I want her with me, so I can protect her."

He didn't ask her from what Elena wanted to keep her daughter safe. He asked only about Stacia. "Do you have a picture of her?"

She reached into her purse and pulled a photo from her wallet. Her heart clenched as she stared down at the image of her daughter's smiling face, her eyes alight with love and excitement as she sat on one of the swings at the park she had so much fun visiting. With a slightly shaking hand, she passed the picture across the desk.

"She's beautiful," Roarke said. "She looks exactly like you."

"I don't have a picture of Kirk." She hadn't carried one of him in years.

"It's fine. I can pull his driver's license picture from the DMV. I'll also run his credit cards—"

"My grandmother gave him some money. Cash. He'll probably use that first."

He sighed, his frustration echoing hers. "So it may be a while before he needs to use his cards."

And a while before Donovan Roarke found Stacia. Damn Joseph. Why had he had to follow that order of Thora's, especially when he'd sensed Kirk's desperation and suspected he might do something crazy? She would never be able to trust him now, even though he'd told her the truth.

"Tell me more about your daughter," he urged her. "Does she wear any jewelry?"

She shook her head. "I never got her any. She plays too hard for jewelry." Apparently even when she wasn't supposed to: jumping rope in the house to show off for Joseph. She'd realized her daughter had had contact with him, but she hadn't known how much, that they'd formed a relationship of sorts.

"No bracelet. Nothing?" he persisted.

She shook her head again. "Why—"

"I ask because I'm making a list of things I can mention to hotel clerks, something they might notice about her."

"She has to have her white teddy bear and her hot-pink fleece blanket or she can't sleep." At least Kirk had taken her special things with them. But why the charm? Unless he hadn't been the one to take it….

She opened her mouth to share that information with Roarke, then changed her mind. She'd already told Joseph too much; she couldn't afford to do the same with this man. She couldn't explain the importance of the charm to a stranger. She hadn't even told Joseph about the charms.

"I'll find her," Roarke assured Elena again.

Reaching into her purse, she retrieved her wallet and scribbled an amount on a check. Like Thora had had Joseph give Kirk, a lot of money.

"Find her fast," she demanded as she passed the check over to him.

He didn't even look at the piece of paper, all his attention focused on Stacia's photo that he still held. "I will."

Only moments ago he'd closed the door behind her, but still his hand shook. He'd touched her. He could have killed her so easily, but it hadn't been time to take her life.

For one, she hadn't had the charm on her. When he'd held her hands, he'd checked her wrists; they'd been bare but for a slim gold watch. Everything about her was classy, so completely different from her earthy mother and whimsical sister.

But he couldn't let her looks deceive him. Despite the cool blond hair and pale eyes, Durikken blood flowed through her veins. Because of that, the McGregor blood meant nothing; it wasn't enough to spare her life—not when he knew she had witchcraft abilities, too. Like her sisters.

The witches had to die. But he couldn't kill her now, not when she might be able to lead him to her daughter. What if her husband called her, demanding more money to return her little girl? He could make the ransom drop, taking both the money and the girl. He'd given her his cell number, scribbling it onto the back of one of his business cards, so he'd know the moment she heard anything about her daughter.

He'd thought taking the little girl would be so easy…when he'd known where she was. *Damn that man!* He struck his fist against the desk. The green shade on his banker's lamp rattled, casting eerie shadows across the open journal on the blotter. He'd patched the spine and managed to save a few pages of the old book, his family history, that the old woman had had locked away in a safe.

She'd told him how the McGregors had changed their name and tried to distance themselves from Eli McGregor, from the killing he'd done. Most of his family thought their ancestor a madman and they had locked away his journal, discounting his writing as the ramblings of a lunatic.

Donovan considered Eli a hero. As he would be

once he killed all the witches. When was that sniveling bastard going to use his credit cards again? Just how much money had the old hag given him? As much as she'd given *him?*

He wouldn't let it matter if Phillips didn't use his credit cards. Donovan would use other ways to track down the little witch. He didn't care about her father, except that the son of a bitch had made it harder for Donovan to carry out his plans.

Anger and frustration ate at him, like the cancer growing inside his head. The doctors had already written him off for dead, saying only a frickin' miracle would save him now. They didn't believe in miracles, but Donovan did.

Three hundred and fifty years ago his ancestor, Eli McGregor, had been struck by lightning and left for dead. But the witch had saved him, using the charms she forged of the lightning-damaged earth, to bring him back to life. Those charms had magical abilities, like the witches who had possession of them.

And he needed them. Now. Then, like Eli, he intended to kill the witches who helped him. As Eli had grown more powerful with the first witch's death, Donovan would grow even more powerful with the deaths of all the witches.

He intended to start with the little witch, but now he had to find her first. But as he'd promised her mother, he *would* find her. Then he'd kill her.

Chapter 7

She opened the door at the barest brush of knuckles against the wood. She'd been waiting, not just for news of her daughter, but for him. She hadn't been able to admit it until she stepped back and let him in.

Elena's heart clenched over the way he looked at her, his jaw taut, only a circle of green rimming his dark pupils. He studied her seriously, intimately, just like he did in her dreams.

"Joseph…"

"I believe you," he said.

Her heart lifted, those three words meaning

more to her than they should. She had to dredge deep to summon the anger she needed to guard against feeling anything else for Joseph Dolce.

"Only because you talked to David. Without his corroboration, you'd still think I'm crazy." She couldn't blame him for what she'd occasionally thought of herself, but she did blame him for giving Kirk the money which had enabled him to take Stacia and remain untraceable.

"I didn't think you were crazy," he said. "I knew something was up last night. You could *see* something I couldn't."

"Something I didn't want to see," she said. Her daughter, scared and alone. Elena's heart beat heavy with dread. God, she hoped she was wrong, that she'd misinterpreted the vision. Maybe what she'd seen was only a game of hide and seek between Kirk and Stacia. Or Joseph and Stacia. She closed her mind to the image of those hands on her little girl's arms, tightening…

"I can't imagine how you must feel seeing these things," he said, his voice thick with emotion, "knowing they're going to happen."

"You said the other day that you haven't felt fear in a long time. I don't remember a time I haven't been afraid," she admitted, her pride be damned. "But I remind myself that my visions are of the future, stuff that hasn't happened yet. I have to make sure it doesn't happen. I have to find her before the killer does, Joseph."

"We will," he promised as he reached for her.

She stepped back before she could give in to the temptation to lay her head on his chest, to let him protect her from all her fears. Maybe she had more in common with Myra Cooper than the ability to see the future. She was like her mother, looking for comfort and security in a man's arms.

His arms, heavy with muscles straining against the rolled-up sleeves of his shirt, would certainly offer her that and probably much more. But she was stronger now than her mother. She didn't need to turn to a man for protection; she could take care of herself. She'd been doing that, as well as taking care of her father, for two decades. She needed Joseph for Stacia, not for herself.

"So how do we find her?" she asked, willing, despite her inability to trust him, to accept his help. She'd talked to Thora. She had David Koster hacking into every system he could to check on Kirk's credit cards, and she'd even hired a private investigator. But somehow she suspected Joseph could accomplish more.

"I have connections I can use," he admitted. "*Influence* I can exert."

"You don't have to play the heavy for me, like you do Thora."

His lips quirked into that wicked grin. "Who says I'm playing?"

She narrowed her eyes. "For some reason I don't think you're the goon you pretend to be."

"Don't make the mistake of thinking I'm something I'm not, Elena. I grew up doing whatever I had to do to survive." Shadows darkened his eyes, shadows of his past and regret for those things he'd had to do. Despite his wealth and power, he still lived in those shadows.

She'd been curious about him for so long, the things she'd heard just fueled her appetite for more…of Joseph. Finally she felt as though she could question him. "What about your parents?"

"I never knew my dad, had a feeling my mom didn't either. Like your mom, she liked men." One of his hands fisted at his side; it was a big hand, the knuckles scarred from old wounds. From fighting. "My mom preferred having the men around to having me around."

She reached for his hand, closing her fingers over the top of his fist. "So she threw you out? How old were you?"

He lowered his head, his gaze focused on the way she held his hand. "Twelve."

The same age she'd been when she'd lost her mom and sisters. Her heart ached for him, for his lost childhood. "Oh, Joseph—"

"No," he said, pulling away from her touch. "Don't feel sorry for me. I did all right. Big house, fast cars, tailored suits."

He didn't mention fancy women again. Did he have one? Probably several with his looks and sex appeal. "But are you happy?" she asked.

He shrugged. "I'm not sure what happy is."

She believed him. "Happy is my little girl's smile, the way it lights up her eyes, her whole face. The way she hugs me as tightly as her arms can wrap around me. She fills up my heart, my soul…" Her breath caught as tears clogged her throat.

Joseph pulled her into his arms. They were as strong as she'd thought. But not comforting. Instead of security, she felt uneasy, on edge, anxious. She tugged free, then brushed a hand across her face, surprised that her palm came away wet from tears leaking out of the corners of her eyes.

"We'll find her," he promised again, offering a confidence she'd never felt, a security she'd never known.

"We have to find her before *he* does."

"Have you had another vision?" he asked.

She shook her head. "Not since last night when I had the two…one of Stacia hiding and then later, one of Kirk…dead." She couldn't mention the blonde, not if there was a chance it was *her.* Then he might try to convince her to leave the search to others, and she couldn't do that. Even though she'd hired a professional, she hoped to find her daughter first.

"But this morning in my office," he said, his brow furrowing, "I could have sworn you had another. You got that faraway, entranced look again."

She stepped away from him, shaking her head as she tried to shake off the remnants of that vision. But she preferred it to the others, which she had to let go of or lose her sanity. She needed a distraction. She needed Joseph. The images, from her morning vision, rolled through her head again; Joseph opening her blouse, then her bra, staring at her breasts. Her heart pounded. "No."

"What did you see, Elena?" he persisted.

Heat rose to her face, then moved lower, spreading throughout her body. Like his touch. She swallowed hard, reminding herself it was just a dream. "Nothing."

"You didn't act like it was *nothing.* You jumped when I touched you." He touched her again, his hand sliding from her shoulder down her arm. She trembled as desire coursed through her. "Like now."

She fought a smile, her irritation that he'd gotten a reaction out of her more with herself than him. "You don't give up, do you?"

"I wouldn't be alive if I was a quitter."

"I didn't intend to tell you anything, and instead I told you—"

"You haven't told me everything. Not yet. But you will." He drew her to him, one hand on her wrist. Then his other hand cupped her cheek, tilting her head up to his. "What did you see this morning, in my office?"

She shook her head. "I'm not going to tell *you*."

"Was it *us?* Like this?" he teased, pulling her closer until her body brushed against the hard, taut length of his.

She shook her head again. She'd already told him far more than she'd intended. He knew more about her than her husband ever had. "Leave me alone, Joseph."

"You shouldn't be alone, Elena." His voice deepened to a sensual growl when he added, "Not a woman like you."

"A woman like me?"

"Beautiful, smart, caring…"

Of all his compliments, the last seemed to impress him the most. Because no one had ever really cared about him…

"Joseph, I'm not going to tell you." *I'd rather show you*. The wicked thought flitted through her mind, but she fought the temptation.

Joseph didn't. His head dipped, his mouth brushing across hers once, twice, before taking it in a deep, intimate kiss. His tongue pushed between her lips, staking claim.

Elena murmured, overcome by the emotions whipping through her. Her skin heated, her pulse raced. She trembled with desire more powerful than anything she'd ever felt before…even in her dreams. And all he'd done was kiss her.

But he tore his mouth from hers and stepped back. His chest rose and fell with his harsh breaths. "God, Elena, I'm sorry—I didn't mean to…"

A smile tugged at her lips. She'd never heard Joseph speak with anything but self-assurance and lethal charm. Until now, when he stammered out an apology over a kiss.

He pushed a slightly shaking hand through his dark hair. "That's not why I came over here."

He'd come to tell her he believed her. No one had ever accepted her so easily. Not even herself. Especially not herself. Of course he'd had to talk to David first. He'd had to have confirmation of her claims. Even though she couldn't blame him, her smile slipped away.

She missed it. The smile. The brief reprieve from the worry that gripped her, that made her unable to sleep. Unable to breathe. Unable to feel anything but fear.

Except for those moments in his arms. Then she'd been caught up in his kiss. In the passion. As she kept reminding herself, her visions were of the future. Stuff that hadn't happened yet. So for tonight, she'd believe Stacia was safe, playing silly games with her father. Laughing, happy.

"Elena, *say* something," he urged her. "*Slap* me. *Do* something."

She closed the distance between them, stood on tiptoe, and pressed her mouth to his. She wanted another reprieve. She wanted to be lost in sensation, not fear. If only for a few stolen moments…

Again Joseph pulled back, his green eyes dilated with passion, his breath ragged. "Elena?"

"Make love to me, Joseph."

"Elena—"

She gripped his shoulders, the muscles bunching beneath her hands. "Joseph, this is how you can help me. Tonight."

A muscle jumped in his cheek, his face stern until she stroked her fingers along the rigid line of his jaw. Then she slid her fingers over his lips, stroking the silky flesh. For such a hard man, his lips were soft. Sensual. She wanted to taste them again. But before she could press her mouth to his, he lifted her.

Then he carried her upstairs, effortlessly, his arms barely straining; hers wrapped around his neck, their mouths tight against each other, fused with passion. Their tongues mated, sliding over each other, slick and sweet. Passion pounded in Elena's veins, so that her heart raced.

She tore her mouth from his. "Joseph…"

Somehow he'd known which room was hers, and he laid her upon her bed, his eyes dark with passion, the pupils eclipsing the green. "I love how you say my name."

For a year she wouldn't use it, had insisted on calling him Mr. Dolce and keeping distance between them. When he followed her onto the bed, his chest pressing down on hers, there was no distance between them anymore. His heart beat hard, echoing the beat of hers.

She wanted nothing between them anymore, not even clothes. She tugged at his tie, undoing the knot and pulling it free of his collar. He stood up, then made short work of the buttons of his shirt, parting the green silk to reveal the firm muscles of his chest, lightly covered with black hair.

She held out her arms, wanting him back. But he shook his head, reaching instead for the buttons of her blouse. His big fingers fumbled with the little mother-of-pearl buttons, his slowness teasing her. She shifted against the bed, the comforter rustling beneath her. His knuckles brushed across her bare skin as he eased apart the blouse.

Her breath hitched, trapped in her lungs, as he

caressed her with just his knuckles gliding along her rib cage below the lace edge of her bra.

"Joseph." She whispered his name now, her voice husky with desire. For him.

His green eyes gleamed as he caressed her with his gaze, too. "Elena, you're so beautiful you take my breath away."

She sat up, winding her arms around his neck as she pressed her mouth against his. She wanted to literally steal his breath, too, as she kissed him deeply, her tongue tangling with his. His chest rose and fell, pushing against her breasts, as his heart beat hard.

For her.

He wanted her…even though he now knew exactly what she was. Cursed.

She slid her mouth from his, gasping for breath. "Make love to me, Joseph," she implored him again.

His lips lifted in his wicked grin. "You just can't resist telling me what to do."

She glanced down, then up again through her lashes, flirting with him and surprised that she remembered how. It had been so long since she'd flirted or done anything else but fight with a man. Doubts tried to steal over her, but she fought them back, refusing to think. Refusing to do anything but feel. "Please…"

He groaned. "When you ask me like that…" His hands on her shoulders, he pushed her none too gently back onto the bed.

"Joseph!" she protested his roughness even as excitement coursed through her veins, heating her blood and her desire for him.

"I'm not tender, Elena. That's not the kind of lover I'll be," he warned her.

She reached for him again, sliding her arms around his back. Muscles rippled beneath his skin, beneath her soft touch. "I know."

"And you don't care?" he teased, as he settled more of his weight onto her, crushing her into the mattress.

Instead of being overwhelmed or intimidated by his size, she felt her pulse race. "I want *you*, Joseph."

He eased up, bracing his hands beside her waist. Muscles bunched and rippled in his bare arms. "I've wanted you for so long…."

"So take me," she said, as if it were all so simple. Nothing was simple, between them, or in her life. But she needed this, stolen moments away from her thoughts and fears. She needed *him*.

He moved back, shifting away from her. Disappointment coursed through her at his distance. Had he changed his mind?

Something thumped against the floor. She

turned her head, following the noise to where his shoe had dropped. Then his other shoe followed. A zipper swished, and his pants dropped onto his shoes.

Her lips curved into a satisfied smile, but he wiped it off with his mouth, kissing her deeply, before pulling back with a complaint. "You're overdressed."

"I can fix that," she offered, lifting up to undo the hook at the waistband of her skirt. Then she slid the zipper down her hip. She raised her gaze, watching passion flare in Joseph's eyes, as she shimmied out of the garment and lay back, wearing only her lace and satin bra and matching panties.

He blew out a ragged breath, stirring the black hair that had fallen across his forehead. "You're testing my control," he warned her.

"What control?" she teased, as she reached out, sliding her fingertips from his collarbone, over his chest and hard, male nipples and lower. The hair of his chest tickled her palms as she ran her hands over him. The hair arrowed down, disappearing into the waistband of his boxers. His erection pressed hard against the cotton material, testing its strength. Before she could reach for him, strong fingers closed around her wrists, tugging her hands away, pushing them above her head as he pressed her back against the mattress.

"Oh, no," he said, his breathing coming harsh through his parted lips. "I may not be gentle, but I'm not that fast."

"You're not easy?" she teased.

He shook his head. "Nothing involving you has ever been easy, Elena."

She drew her bottom lip between her teeth, gnawing at it while she acknowledged the truth of what he claimed. Nothing in her life had ever been easy. Why did this feel easy? Why did it feel right to lie in his arms, beneath his hard body, when it couldn't be more complicated?

"Joseph…"

"No," he said, speaking to her thoughts. "We're not stopping now. I'm not a gentleman who can hop in a cold shower and pretend we never got this far."

"I don't want to stop." She just wanted to forget everything else, everything that complicated her life. "But I bet you would if I asked."

He caught her chin in one hand while he held her wrists together, above her head, with his other hand. "Don't," he commanded her, as he exerted pressure on her face.

She lifted a brow. "What?"

"Don't think I'm something I'm not," he threatened her, his green eyes hard and serious. "Don't mistake me for some white knight who's going to rescue you."

A giggle slipped from between her lips. "Don't worry, Joseph. No one would ever mistake you for a white knight."

And she didn't want to be rescued. She intended to do the rescuing herself. She'd find the strength, maybe in his arms, not from him but from deep within herself.

"No," he agreed, expelling a breath of obvious relief. "No one would."

Perhaps to demonstrate how ungentlemanly he was, he tightened his hold on her wrists, arching her body toward his. Then he slid his free hand from her chin, along her throat to her breasts. He traced the mounds spilling over the satin cups, his fingertips rough, before he undid the front clasp.

She bowed off the bed, lifting her breasts for his attention. Chuckling at her action, he closed his lips around a nipple, tugging at the hard peak.

Passion knotted Elena's stomach, frustration building, as he played her. His tongue lapped at one breast while he stroked the other with his fingertips, running the pad of his thumb over and over the hardened nipple.

Even biting her lip, a cry slipped from her throat. "Joseph, please…"

He finally released her wrists as he moved farther down her body, his soft hair brushing over her breasts, then her rib cage, then her navel. She shivered at the delicious sensation before reaching for him, delving her fingers into his hair. But he refused to move back up her body.

The satin dug into her hip, as he tugged at her panties, tearing the fabric from her. Then his mouth moved between her legs, his breath hot against her most intimate core.

She squirmed and protested, "Joseph..."

But his hands closed around her hips, holding her still as he lapped at her, teasing her with his tongue.

She threw her head back, moans rippling from her throat. He released one hip, stroking his hand up her body until it closed over her breast, squeezing her swollen flesh. He continued his intimate invasion, his tongue sliding in and out of her until she could handle the sweet torture no more. She flew apart, ecstasy shuddering through her in crashing waves.

"Joseph," she panted. He didn't let her catch her breath before he was kissing her, pushing his tongue between her lips, sharing with her the sweetness of her pleasure.

She raked her nails down his back. "Joseph, I want you. Now!"

He pushed her legs apart, then impaled her, sliding his hard erection into her wet heat. Like everything else about him, his penis was so big it should have been intimidating. It stretched her, reaching places inside of Elena never touched before. She whimpered at the pressure, then shifted to accept him. All of him. He drove deeper, then pulled out, sliding in and out. She wrapped her legs around his waist, holding tight as he pumped into her. Guttural groans ripped from his throat, where the cords stood out from his exertion. From his loss of control.

Thrills shot through Elena with his possession. Waves of pleasure crashed through her again as she lost control, the orgasms torn from her.

Joseph clutched her close, his hold almost painful as he shouted his pleasure and buried himself deep inside her. "Oh, Elena…"

His breath coming in harsh pants against her throat, he rolled to his side, keeping them joined, as if he never intended to let her go. She fell asleep that way, as part of him.

Elena's lungs burned as she struggled for breath. But she couldn't open her mouth; water already flowed into her nose and down her throat, drowning her. She kicked out, fighting against the ropes that bound her ankles and pulled her under water. The shaft around which the rope was anchored turned, giving her enough slack to break the surface. Sputtering, she dragged air into her oxygen-deprived lungs, but she managed only one breath before the crank turned forward and pulled her beneath the water again.

She flailed her arms, clawing at the wooden sides of the vat in which she was submerged. Slivers impaled her fingertips, digging deep into the skin. Pain and fear pressed on her chest, like the water, stealing her breath.

Blood pounding in her ears, she heard not even the gurgle of water until the rope slackened around her ankles and she broke free of the surface again. Screams rent the air. Not hers. Her throat burned as she gasped for breath.

"Mommy! Mommy!"

She blinked away the water running from her hair into her eyes and focused on the metal catwalk above the vat. Lack of oxygen clouded her vision, so the images wavered: a figure in a hooded brown robe, a little blond girl clutched in his arms. She wriggled, trying to break free of his grasp.

"Mommy! Don't hurt my mommy!"

Elena clawed her way to the top of the vat near the catwalk, then reached up. "Stacia," she cried, her voice a hoarse croak. "Stacia…"

The man handed the child to Elena, dropping her into the water with her. But as Stacia fell, she grasped the man's robe, pulling the hood free of his face.

And Elena, after months of witnessing his murders, finally saw the killer's face. "No!"

Chapter 8

"Elena, wake up! Honey, wake up!" Strong arms wrapped around her, pulling her close. Fingers tunneled into her hair, pushing it back from her face. "It's okay. You're safe."

Elena wiped her tears on the mat of soft hair covering the chest beneath her cheek. Her breath shuddered out. "Just a dream. It was just a dream…."

"No, it wasn't," Joseph said, refusing to accept the lie she'd often told her husband.

No, it wasn't a dream. None of it. Not making love with him and not what she'd just seen inside her head. But he'd lied to her, too, because he couldn't help her, couldn't keep her safe. She'd never be safe, not even in Joseph's arms. Maybe especially not in Joseph's arms.

What the hell had she been thinking? Of course, she hadn't been. She hadn't wanted to think. She'd wanted to escape her thoughts, her fears, but she'd only raised more. She pulled away, sat up, raised her knees, and wrapped her arms around them.

"You're doing it again," he said.

Pulling away? She should have done that sooner, before he wound up in her bed. Even though she'd filed, she wasn't divorced yet, and after her disaster of a marriage, she'd be a fool to trust any man again—especially not a man like Joseph. Not a man for whom money and power meant more than integrity and honor. They had no future.

She had no future, not if her vision came to pass. And what about her daughter? How could she have, for even a moment, put Stacia out of her mind?

Joseph's voice rumbled close to her ear. "You're holding yourself together."

A shrill little laugh slipped out as she neared hysteria. "Barely."

"What did you *see*, Elena? Tell me."

"The killer." Her breath hitched, as his face flashed into her mind again. "I saw the killer."

"You've seen the killer before."

David had obviously told him everything. "In a brown robe, with the hood raised. I've never seen his face. Until just now."

"What does he look like?"

She reminded herself that her visions didn't always give her the total picture of what was actually happening. "I can't be sure it's him. I thought I had a vision of the killer before. I thought *David* was the killer. Maybe I misinterpreted what I saw this time, too."

"What did you see?" Joseph asked again, his hands closing over her bare shoulders, his palms warm against her skin.

"I was drowning." Her throat and the back of her nose burned from water, as if she'd really been submerged. "Someone was drowning me. And he had Stacia."

Joseph pulled her back against his chest, wrapping his arms around her. Skin pressed to skin, reminding Elena of where they were…in bed and what they'd done. How had she lost control, how had she forgotten not only who she was, a distraught mother, but who Joseph was, a man she couldn't trust?

"You saw the killer then," he said.

"I think." She shook her head. "I don't know. Maybe he was there because he was saving me, like David was actually saving Ariel."

Play The Lucky Hearts Game

and get...
FREE BOOKS & a FREE GIFT...
YOURS to KEEP!

Yes! I have scratched off the silver card. Please send me my **FREE BOOKS** and **FREE MYSTERY GIFT**. I understand that I am under no obligation to purchase any books as explained on the back of this card. I am over 18 years of age.

Scratch Here! then look below to see what you can claim...

I8II8

Mrs/Miss/Ms/Mr _____ Initials _____

BLOCK CAPITALS PLEASE

Surname _____

Address _____

_____

Postcode _____

Twenty-one gets you
4 FREE BOOKS and a **MYSTERY GIFT!**

Twenty gets you
1 FREE BOOK and a **MYSTERY GIFT!**

Nineteen gets you
1 FREE BOOK!

TRY AGAIN!

The Mills & Boon® Book Club™ — Here's how it works:

THE MILLS & BOON® BOOK CLUB™
FREE BOOK OFFER
FREEPOST CN81
CROYDON
CR9 3WZ

NO STAMP
NECESSARY
IF POSTED IN
THE U.K. OR N.I.

"You know him," Joseph deduced. "Is it Kirk?"

"No. When this vision happens, Kirk's probably already dead." Not that her visions ever followed any consequential order. Or any order at all.

"Then who's the man?"

She swallowed hard, forcing down her panic, as in her mind, the hood fell back, revealing mahogany hair, graying at the temples, and deep brown eyes. "Donovan Roarke, the private investigator I hired to find Stacia."

Joseph expelled a ragged breath, which was warm against her neck. "You hired an investigator?"

God, what if she'd actually hired the killer? No, she must have misinterpreted the vision. "I had to do everything possible to find Stacia."

His chest pushed against her back, soft hair brushing her bare skin, as he drew in a deep breath. "Then why don't you…"

She turned toward him, tilting her head to meet his gaze as he hesitated. "Why don't I what?"

His green eyes softened with sympathy. "Why don't you *use* your gift?"

"Curse," she automatically corrected him. "I have no control over it. I can't force these visions." She couldn't even force them away, despite how hard she'd tried the past twenty years.

"David said you used a vision to find Ariel a few

weeks ago." He squeezed her shoulders as if lending her strength. "Use your visions now, Elena."

"How? I can barely make sense of them. Sometimes I think it's me in the vision even when I know it must be Irina, or someone else. I don't always know or understand what I've seen. I got lucky when I had the vision of Ariel. I understood that one." Maybe if she had the charm she'd be able to figure out more of her visions; she'd been holding the little star the night she had the vision of Ariel that had led her to the church where David, Ty and Ariel had battled the killer. But the charm was gone…like Stacia. Her heart lurched as fear for her daughter's safety intensified. It had never really been gone, even while she'd made love to Joseph; that hollow feeling in her chest remained, the hole in her heart that ached over the loss of her baby.

"Try," Joseph urged her.

"The vision I had of Kirk…" She squeezed her eyes shut, trying to recall the grisly image of her husband lying dead on a motel room floor.

"What do you remember of it?" he prodded.

"He's lying beside a bed, on threadbare carpet. If you gave him that much money, why would he be staying in a sleazy motel?" The vision had to be wrong, or she'd misconstrued it. Maybe she saw something that happened years from now, when Kirk had run through all the money.

"That makes sense. Most hotels and reputable motels are going to want a credit card for a deposit."

"And he doesn't want to be found, so he won't use his cards. How do we find him, Joseph?" Panic pressed on her chest, stealing her breath like the water had. "How do we find my daughter before the killer does?"

"Tell me what else you saw. What's Kirk wearing? What else do you see?"

She tightened her arms around her knees, so that she wouldn't tremble. If she lost control, she couldn't help anyone. She'd proved that by sleeping with Joseph. "He's covered in blood, with neon light flashing across him."

"Neon light? From a sign? Did you see the sign?"

She shook her head. "Only the light flashing across him…" She concentrated on the memory of the images from that vision, on the neon flashing across his chest. "Backwards letters. Something…Inn." Tears of frustration burned her eyes. "I don't know."

Joseph tensed. "The private investigator—tell me his name again?"

"Donovan Roarke. Thora used him before. Do you know him?"

He shook his head. "No. But my secretary said a man was in the office today, asking about Kirk. He found out about Felicia."

"You already know about her."

"And I told Koster. We're watching her credit cards, too."

"But Kirk probably won't let her use hers either."

He was being careful, which was uncharacteristic for him. Did he know about the witch hunt as well as Elena's curse?

"Maybe. But he won't be able to stop her from using her phone. I checked the logs for her direct line today." He glanced at his watch and corrected himself, "Yesterday. And she spends a lot of time on the phone."

"You think she might have called someone? Who?"

"I'll check the log again. Talk to the people she talked to. She might have called a friend—"

"A sister." For the past twenty years, that was all Elena had wanted to do, talk to her sisters again. Now she ached to talk to her daughter again, to hold her in her arms, to protect her from the evil stalking them.

Joseph pulled into the parking lot, which was awash with light from the blue-and-orange neon Lancaster Inn sign. This was where, after some coercion, Felicia's sister had sent them. She'd been reluctant to reveal their whereabouts because Kirk was hiding from his frigid wife and some guy who'd threatened him. She hadn't known Elena was his wife, Joseph the threat. They'd posed as Felicia's coworkers, who had a severance check to bring her. Joseph had even produced an official company payroll check to support his story, so she hadn't questioned the late hour or their desperation as much as she should have.

Regrettably she'd admitted that she'd already talked to someone else, a private investigator, but she hadn't told him where to find her sister. Was Elena's vision right? Was the private investigator she'd hired a killer?

For her sake and Stacia's, he hoped not. He shut off the engine. "Okay, you wait here."

"I'm going, too."

He shook his head. "Don't worry, you'll be right here." Which probably wasn't the greatest idea either, to leave her alone in the parking lot. On the long drive to Lancaster, he was pretty sure he'd lost the guards Koster had assured Joseph he had following Elena. Her fear and urgency, after her last vision, was so intense, he'd become swept up in it, too. He'd driven fast and a bit recklessly in his haste to get to Stacia. "You stay here, with the doors locked, and I'll bring Stacia to you."

Elena bit her lip as tears shone in her pale eyes. But she blinked them back, too strong to cry. "I'm going." She threw open her door. "She's *my* daughter, Joseph."

And if something had happened to her, she wanted to know. She *had* to know. He understood and nodded reluctantly.

"Okay, but stay behind me," he said as they climbed the stairs to the third floor. Although he didn't have any psychic abilities, he had an uneasy feeling. The hair lifted on the nape of his neck, and his gut churned.

He'd never messed with guns. With his muscle, he hadn't had to, but all of a sudden he wished he had one. What if Elena's vision had already come true? The door of room 323B was partially open. No light spilled out from within; the room was completely dark but for the flashing of the neon sign.

Joseph grabbed Elena's arm and dragged her back toward the stairs. "Go to the truck and wait for me."

"The door's open," she said, even though she wouldn't have been able to see around him. Had she had another vision of her husband's murder scene?

"Go back," he ordered. Then he closed his fingers around the handle of the switchblade he'd carried since he was a kid. It wasn't a gun, but it had protected him more than once.

Elena's protest was just a shake of her head, but from the determination burning bright in her pale eyes, he knew he wasn't going to be able to budge her, not unless he threw her over his shoulder and carried her back to his Navigator. And he didn't dare take the time.

"It's already happened." Her voice cracked with emotion, her throat moving as she swallowed hard. "My vision has already come true."

"We don't know that. They could have left it open while they went to get ice," he reasoned. But his argument fell flat. He didn't believe that anymore than she did.

"She's my daughter, Joseph. I have to…"

He took a deep breath, then turned back toward the room, and pushed the door open the rest of the way.

"Stacia," Elena called out. "Stacia?"

Joseph reached inside, flipping on the light switch by the door. The lamps beside the bed illuminated the bloody sheets and pillows. Kirk's body, clad only in silk pajama bottoms, lay on the floor, his face and chest spattered with blood, which pooled beneath him. At the foot of the bed, a woman lay on her side, her blond hair, matted with blood, stuck to her face.

Joseph glanced back toward Elena, who had followed him into the room. She held a hand across her mouth, holding in a scream. She'd already seen this once, inside her head. God, he couldn't imagine the horror of her visions. He kept his gaze on Elena, averting it from the gruesome scene.

"Stacia." He called the little girl's name now, his voice cracking. "Stacia?"

Tears slid down Elena's face and over the hand pressed to her mouth.

"She's not here," he said.

She pointed toward a closed door. The bathroom door stood open; it wasn't that. A connecting room? He tried the knob, which turned easily in his hand.

"Stacia?" he called out.

A lamp glowed beside the bed, its bulb dim.

"She always has to have a night-light," Elena said, "she's scared of the dark."

After what he'd just seen, Joseph had a feeling he might be from now on, too. "She's not here," he said.

Her voice a horrified whisper, she murmured, "He has her...."

Joseph grabbed her, squeezing her shoulders. "No, Elena. We don't know that. She probably ran when she heard the shots."

But if anyone had heard the shots, someone would have called the police. God, this killer was clever. He must have used a silencer. If the little girl had been sleeping, she wouldn't have heard anything...until it was too late.

Elena jerked from his grasp, then dropped to her

knees before he could grab her again. She doubled over, and Joseph's heart ached for her pain. Then she lifted the blankets and peered under the bed. When she reached her arms underneath, his heart lifted with hope.

She'd hidden. Somehow she'd known the danger was close, and she'd hid. But Elena dragged out only a bedraggled teddy bear, not a little girl. But she had been under there, hiding. Had she hid long enough, then gone for help?

Joseph reached for the closet door, glancing inside; only a few clothes swung from the rod, miniature shirts and pants in the bright colors Stacia loved. His gut twisted. "We have to look for her. She might be hiding somewhere else, maybe outside."

This room had a door to the outside, too. She could have run out when she heard the killer coming. She was a smart kid. God, he hoped that she had run.

"She's gone," Elena said, her voice shaking, as she remained kneeling on the floor, running her hands over the carpet under the bed. "The charm's gone, too." Her breath audibly caught. "He has the little star charm and my daughter."

Koster had filled him in on the charms. Ariel figured bringing them together again would stop the witch hunt, that having one could protect the person who held it from harm. "Stacia has it with her. That's good," he tried to assure her. But he couldn't help but think that Elena didn't have anything for protection…but him.

He'd never had anyone count on him…but him.

In the distance, sirens whined, getting louder and louder. Someone must have heard the shots after all. "God, this just happened." His heart pounded and sweat dampened his palms as if he was a street kid again, about to be picked up. "Come on, we have to get out of here," he said.

She glanced up at him, her eyes dazed. "What? Why? What are you—"

His heart ached for the pain and loss on her beautiful face. "Elena, if they find us here, with Kirk and his mistress dead in there, the police are going to think *we* shot them."

"But we didn't—"

"By the time we explain that to them—"

"Stacia could be dead, too." She stood up. "You're right. We have to get out of here."

They went out the door of the room where Stacia had hidden under the bed, but as they passed the other room, Joseph glanced through the open door, at the little girl's father lying there, all bloody. Joseph had already believed Elena that there was a killer after her, but he hadn't realized just how close the guy had gotten.

He reached for Elena, wrapping his arm tight around her shoulders as they ran down the stairs. She clutched Stacia's bear tight, probably wishing that she'd held her daughter as closely so that Kirk had never been able to take her.

All her fears were being realized. Kirk hadn't been strong enough to protect her little girl, and the killer had beaten them to Stacia.

Now could they beat the killer before he hurt the little girl? Could Joseph become that white knight Elena needed to save her daughter and herself?

Elena held tight to the phone cord as her knees weakened, and she sagged against the side of the phone booth. The skin of her legs stuck to the thick, clear plastic wall. Despite being late spring, the night air had cooled, chilling her legs, bare below the hem of her skirt. Even though she wore a sweater with the skirt, she couldn't stop shivering.

"Answer, answer," she pleaded as she listened to the ringing.

Then a sleepily mumbled, "Hello?"

"Ariel?"

"Elena, what's happened?" Her sister was instantly awake and anxious.

"Is she there?" Elena asked, her voice breaking,

as she imagined her little girl as a ghost that only her sister could see.

"Who? Oh, God, not Stacia…"

"Is she?" Elena yelled, her grasp on control slipping fast. She clutched the teddy bear to her side, holding it as tightly as she wished she'd held her daughter. "Tell me, is my baby dead?"

"No, honey, I don't see her."

"But that doesn't mean that she's not…"

"No, it does," Ariel insisted. "If my niece were dead, she'd seek me out, Elena. She knows me. She has the gift, you know. She can see ghosts, too."

"That day on the playground." During one of the first meetings between the sisters, Stacia had seen a girl on the swings that Elena hadn't been able to see. She hadn't been an imaginary friend, not if Ariel had seen her.

"She saw a ghost that day." Elena voiced the fear she'd denied until now. Her daughter was cursed, like them. She had her aunt's ability *and* her mother's. She'd seen Kirk and his friend's deaths…before they'd ever happened. Before Elena had seen them.

"Yes. And I think that's where Mama is. I think she's with Stacia. Between her and the charm, they'll keep her safe," her sister assured her. "She still has the charm, right?"

Either her or the killer. "I didn't find it in the hotel room where we found the bodies."

"Bodies?" her sister gasped.

Elena nodded, then realized her sister couldn't see her action. "Yes. Kirk and his mistress. They were murdered, Ariel. Shot to death. And Stacia's gone."

"Oh, my God! Are you all right?"

Scared out of her mind. Guilt-ridden. A million emotions assailed Elena. Her baby was missing. And Kirk and his friend hadn't deserved to die. Shame for wishing him gone, for wishing him harm, weighed on her. But she couldn't deal with anything now but the search for her daughter.

"The police might contact you, looking for me. That's why I'm calling from a pay phone, not my cell." She'd also needed a moment alone, a moment to collect herself…and plan her next move.

"So they can't trace the call? My God, what's going on, Elena? Come here, and we'll get this all sorted out with the police. We'll explain—"

"There's no time," she interrupted her sister. "I need to find Stacia. Now. *He* has her. *He* has my daughter."

"She's alive. I'm sure of it," Ariel insisted.

Elena drew in the first unrestricted breath she'd taken since finding her husband and his mistress dead. Ariel was right; Stacia would seek out her aunt…if she'd passed away. She was alive. For now…

"Listen, I don't have much time," Elena said, glancing toward the black SUV parked by the curb. The tinted windows hid Joseph from her view, but not her from his. She had to be careful. "Have David and Ty check out Donovan Roarke."

"Who is he?"

"He may be the killer." God, she hoped she was wrong. She hoped, like before, that she'd misinterpreted her vision. But she had a horrible feeling, as his face flashed through her mind again, the hood falling back, that she was right. "He might have Stacia."

"Elena—"

"I have to go," she said, hanging up the phone on her sister. She could have given her more information, more details about Donovan Roarke, but Elena had one more call to make, quickly.

She fumbled in her pocket for the business card she'd shoved there. She pulled it out and held it in the faint light of the street lamp, turning it over to read the cell number scribbled across the back. With shaking fingers, she fed the pay phone a couple more quarters. Then she punched in the numbers on the card. Ringing echoed in her ear and inside her head.

Then the lightning flashed, both in her mind, and in the predawn sky. Thunder rumbled in the distance, like gunfire, and raindrops spattered the sides of the phone booth, obscuring her vision of Joseph's black SUV.

But she saw him somewhere else, on a dirty cement floor, blood spilling from his body.

Her heart clenched in her chest, hurting.

Would there be no end to the killing? Would everyone she cared about die?

Chapter 9

"No one saw us at the hotel," Joseph said, as he drove back toward Barrett. Despite his assurance to Elena, he knew it wouldn't take the police long to track him down. Once Felicia's sister admitted to telling him where Kirk was, Joseph would become the prime suspect. During his years as a street kid, he'd had too many scrapes with the law. Not to mention he'd threatened Kirk and then slept with the guy's wife.

If he were the police, he'd suspect himself, too. He had more motive than anyone else for killing Kirk.

"Nobody will blame you for the murders," she said, offering *him* reassurance. "You have an alibi."

Her. He could taste her yet on his lips, feel her skin pressed hotly against his. He shook his head. "Being each other's alibis doesn't help us."

"Jail's the least of my concerns," she said.

"We'll find her." That was all he could promise, after seeing the killer's other victims. His gut twisted, nerves churning. Although he hadn't felt it in years, he recognized the sick taste of fear in his mouth and beating within his heart. God, they had to find Stacia alive. Who'd be capable of hurting such a sweet child?

The same sick bastard who could burn a woman alive.

"Where do you want me to bring you?" he asked, as the headlights glinted off the first exit for Barrett. "To your sister's?"

"Where are *you* going?" she asked.

"I've got some things to do." Like track down Donovan Roarke.

"I don't want you involved anymore," she said.

"What?" When she'd known her daughter was with her father, she'd asked for his help. Now, when Stacia was probably with a killer, Elena wanted him to back off? "What the hell's going on?"

Her voice chilled, taking on that icy quality that

had always irritated and fascinated him. "I don't need your help," she insisted.

"Bullshit!"

Her reflection, on the windshield, winced at his curse. Her eyes glowed eerily, that pale blue, in her ashen face. "Asking for your help…it was a mistake." Her breath caught. "Not the only mistake I made with you…"

He winced now as guilt surged through him. He'd like to beat himself up for taking advantage of her when she'd been most vulnerable. But guilt wasn't going to help either one of them. "Elena…"

"While we were…my daughter was hiding from a killer." Her voice cracked. "She needed me most, and I wasn't there for her."

"Elena, that wasn't your fault." It was his.

When he'd gone to see her, he'd had Felicia's call log with him; he'd intended to show her the phone numbers, to contact the people and try to find Kirk and Felicia. But then he'd kissed her…and lost all his good intentions, common sense and control. And because of that, a little girl might lose her life. He couldn't blame Elena if she never forgave him; he doubted he'd ever forgive himself.

"Take me to the estate," she said.

He shook his head. "The police might be there, waiting for you." To arrest her for her husband's and his mistress's murders. "Let me take you to

your sister's. You called her—she knows what's
going on. She'll cover for you."

"No."

God, she was stubborn. With one hand gripping
the wheel, he reached across her with the other.
She shrank back against the seat, as if repulsed by
his closeness. She already hated him.

He clicked open the glove box and pulled out
the cell phone he'd tried to give her earlier. But she
had refused his help then, too, having him stop at
a pay phone instead. Or maybe she'd had another
reason for not wanting to use his untraceable cell.
Revulsion.

"You know why I have this," he said, holding
the cell phone aloft.

Her lips tightened as she nodded. "To do
Thora's dirty work."

"It's not like you think," he said.

But hell, maybe it was. The veiled threats and
the pressure he exerted on business adversaries or
associates to get the deals or the sales Thora
wanted. Basically extortion, and that was why he
hadn't wanted any of the calls traced back to him.
He didn't want to go to jail again, so he'd been
careful about covering his tracks. Until Kirk's and
Felicia's murders, Thora had been the only one
who could send him there, but maybe she'd sent
him to hell instead.

He blew out a ragged breath. "Hell, it's probably worse."

"Joseph." Elena's voice softened on his name. "You're a better man than you think you are."

He shook his head. "I've hurt people, Elena. Not like the killer has but…I've hurt people." He had hurt her. Last night when he'd taken advantage of her.

"Joseph…"

He glanced at her, his heart lifting at the compassion swirling in her eyes along with something else. She wasn't as repulsed by him as he'd thought. Something else was going on with her.

He tapped in the number to Koster's private line; he'd called him once already, when Elena had been in the phone booth. The guy picked up on the first ring. "Dolce?"

"Elena and I are heading back toward Barrett. Is it safe?"

"For now. I checked in with the Lancaster authorities. There was no ID in the hotel. They checked in under aliases."

"So no one knows who they are?"

"Not yet."

That would buy Joseph some time, but not much, before the police were after him. "So it's clear?"

"For now. You really shouldn't have shaken my guys on the way there," Koster admonished him.

"They could have been witnesses. Backup if you needed it."

It had been too late for backup then. Joseph had a feeling he might need it again, though, once he tracked down Roarke. "Where are they now?"

"Back at the estate."

"Keep them there. Elena wants to go home." Although she hadn't called it that. Was that another thing they had in common, growing up as they had, that they never felt as though they'd had a home?

"Not here? Ariel's worried about her."

Ariel wasn't the only one.

"I'll call you back." When Elena wasn't listening and he could tell the other man about his suspicions that something else was going on with her. Joseph pressed the end button, terminating the call, then turned toward Elena. "They haven't identified their bodies yet."

"Then drop me off at the estate," she imperiously directed him, as if nothing had changed between them over the past couple of days, as if he'd never held her in his arms, as if they'd never made love. Maybe she could forget.

But he couldn't.

He held his silence until he pulled through the gates of the estate, but when she reached for the door handle, he caught her arm. "You're not going anywhere, not until you tell me what the hell's going on!"

She lifted her chin, and her eyes iced over like her voice. "When I asked for your help, I made a mistake—"

"We made love," he reminded her.

Her lips tightened. "And we shouldn't have. Look what happened while we…"

"Elena, we had no way of knowing. It's not your fault." Just his.

She shook her head, unwilling to accept his assurances or his help. But there was something else going on, he was certain of it.

She turned her head away, staring out the window instead of meeting his gaze. "I don't want you involved any deeper—"

He pulled her close, pressing her breasts into his chest while he took her mouth in a possessive kiss, sweeping his tongue between her soft lips to claim her as his. Just as his body had claimed hers mere hours ago. Panting, he lifted his head. "I've been buried deep inside you."

And he'd forever be a part of her now. The thought shook him nearly as much as the thought of her little girl at the mercy of a killer. Because he hadn't acted fast enough?

"I care about you and Stacia," he admitted. And he'd never really cared about anyone but himself before. "I'm not going anywhere, Elena. You're not getting rid of me."

"*He* might," she said, her voice a soft quaver as she stared up at him, her pale eyes wide with fear.

"Roarke?"

"I don't know, not for sure." Her breath hitched, then she continued, "But I see you dead. Like Kirk, bleeding to death on a floor." She slid her hands up his shoulders to the nape of his neck, her fingers delving into his hair. "I don't want you getting hurt, Joseph."

"I've been taking care of myself for a long time, Elena." But her caring about him twisted something in his heart, reminding him that he still had one. Or he must have for he'd given it to her. And for the first time he lied to her: "I'll be fine."

But he wouldn't be. Not if something happened to her or her daughter. He understood now why he'd gone so long without caring about anyone. It hurt too damned much.

He glanced out the window, to where a white van was parked across the street. Tinted windows concealed the interior, but he'd noted the plate as he'd driven up, so he had no doubt Koster's guards were inside the van. She'd be safe here, within the estate. Physically. Knowing an animal had her daughter, she wouldn't be emotionally or mentally safe…until she held her daughter again.

He tightened his arms around her, wanting to hold her together instead of watching her do it herself, as she'd done for so many years. Alone.

But he had to go. He had to find Stacia for her. For himself. The thought of the little girl in harm's way twisted his guts into painful knots.

"I have to go," he said, but he couldn't release her. Not yet.

Her breath sighed out against his throat, as she pressed her face into his neck. "Promise me, promise me you won't get hurt, Joseph."

His fingers tunneled into the softness of her hair, holding her close against his heart. And he lied to her again. "Nothing's going to happen to me. I promise."

But it already had. He'd fallen in love with a woman in danger, and her pain was his.

"I told you already. I don't know where your daughter is." Thora leaned back in her chair and stared at the glowing tip of her cigar.

"But you know who took her."

Thora snorted, as if disgusted with Elena's stupidity. "Her father—"

"Kirk had her for a little while. But the killer has her now. You know who that is." Elena studied her grandmother's bent head, her suspicions growing over how the woman, who'd once delighted in staring Elena down, refused to meet her gaze. "You know all about who started the witch hunt again."

Part of Elena had always suspected Thora had something to do with it, from the moment she'd had that first vision of her mother dying in a fire. But Elena hadn't wanted to believe that her grandmother could be that purely evil. She'd given birth to Elena's father, a dear, sweet man, surely she had to have some decency…

"You're talking crazy again," Thora said, still staring intently at the cigar.

"And you're avoiding looking at me. I've noticed that for a while now," Elena realized. "Actually since my father died. Do you hate me that much?"

"Yes!" Thora shouted as she leapt to her feet. "I hate what you are. I hate that my son loved your mother. I hate that he loved *you*."

"You selfish, stupid bitch," Elena hurled the insult. "Didn't you know him at all?"

"She broke him—"

"Because she knew you would never let him be with her, a Durikken descendant." Elijah had told her that himself, just before he'd died. "You may have changed your name, but you didn't drop the vendetta, not really."

Elena shook her head, more disgusted than

afraid of this madwoman, despite all the years Thora had persecuted her with her insults and threats. "And my father's body might have been broken, but his heart was strong. He had enough love for all of us."

Thora dropped back into her chair, weakened by the very thing that had once made her so powerful—her hatred.

"*You* started the witch hunt again," Elena accused her, her stomach churning with dread and fear.

The older woman shook her head. "You don't know what you're talking about."

"I thought he didn't know. I thought it was the fever that had my father rambling incoherently. But now I realize what he was telling me. He met my mother because *you* sent him to find her." Elena had preferred Ariel's romantic scenario, that her parents had met because her father had sought her out to apologize for the vendetta. That would have been an action of the man Elena had known and loved.

Her voice thick with emotion, she accused, "You sent him to kill her."

Thora weakly protested, "Not kill her…"

"What? Just make her life miserable?"

"I wanted to find them. I wanted the *charms*," Thora admitted, her voice rising. "They belong to McGregors, not Durikkens. That was what I sent your father to do, retrieve our property, not fall in love with a witch."

Elena gnawed at her bottom lip before saying, "Not to have me."

"God, no."

If it wasn't all so sick and disgusting, Elena would have laughed at the irony. Instead she stated the obvious, "But my father didn't bring back the charms."

"No." Thora sniffed, unable to accept her son was capable of failure. "She bewitched him, so he forgot his purpose. So he forgot his heritage."

Elena lifted her chin, with pride in her father. "He was no killer."

"I didn't ask him to kill her," Thora insisted, shrilly. "He was supposed to get the charms. That was all." Not a daughter.

The old woman continued, "God, I wished he would have. He needed them when he got sick. They could have healed him. They could have saved him."

Thora didn't believe in witches but she believed in the charms having magical powers? Elena wasn't the only one who'd lied to herself for a long time.

"So you sent someone else after the charms."

Thora nodded. "Over the years. But none of them could track down your mother. With her abilities, they weren't able to find her. That was when I realized that only a McGregor could."

"That's why you didn't use Joseph."

"He wouldn't understand. A man like him, he has no history. He doesn't even know his father's name," she said as if repulsed. "He can't comprehend a history like ours."

"Sick and sordid. I can't comprehend it either," Elena admitted. "But you found a McGregor who did."

Thora blinked hard, but still moisture clouded her eyes. "But it took me too long to find another living McGregor descendent. It was too late for your father."

"Why didn't you just let it go then?" Elena wondered. If Thora had, Myra Cooper and her sisters would still be alive.

"I wanted the charms back."

"For yourself? In case you ever got sick?" Elena laughed now. "God, Thora, you'd have to be human in order to have human frailties."

"The charms belong to the McGregors," the old woman insisted. "There are so few of us left. And I'm the only one who knew the whole history."

"You gave him Eli's journal." That was why it was missing from the safe.

Thora nodded. "So he'd understand how powerful the charms are."

"You told him to use whatever means necessary to retrieve them, even murder?" The horror of it, of having lived with someone capable of this madness for twenty years, overwhelmed Elena. She'd had her child in this house, near this woman.

Thora bit her lip and shook her head. "He wasn't supposed to kill anyone. The witch hunt didn't have to be about killing. It was just about the charms. They belong to McGregors, not Durikkens."

Elena slammed both her fists onto the desk. "He has my daughter!"

Thora's face paled, and she insisted, "He wouldn't hurt Stacia. She's a McGregor, too."

"Donovan Roarke doesn't care," Elena informed her. He'd had no problem killing Kirk and Felicia, and they weren't witches. In deference to that, though, he'd at least skipped the torture.

But maybe the McGregor name did mean something to him, enough to keep him from harming her little girl. Elena had to hang onto that hope…if she had any hope of hanging on to her sanity.

"You know Donovan Roarke?" Thora asked, her eyes wide with shock and more than a trace of fear.

Elena, sick to her stomach, nodded. "I found his card in your desk and hired him to find her. I thought since you used him, he had to be the best."

And he was; he'd beat her and Joseph to Kirk, Felicia and…Stacia.

"He's crazy, Elena," her grandmother said,

using Elena's full first name for the first time ever; obviously so distraught she'd forgotten how much she hated it. "He's taken all of this too far. I think he's sick."

"You think? He's killing people."

The image flashed in her mind again, Joseph lying on that cement floor, his green eyes open. Despite his claim of feeling no fear, his eyes were wide and bright with the emotion. Somehow she suspected it wasn't for himself he was afraid, even as he died. He was afraid for Stacia…and her.

She murmured, "Joseph…"

She should have told him she loved him…even though she just realized it herself. That was why she'd tried to pull away from him, why she'd try to get him to abandon the search, so he wouldn't get hurt. But she'd hurt him by pulling away, by pushing her guilt off on him. Their making love hadn't been his mistake; it had been hers.

"Joseph's helping you?" Thora asked. "He'll find her," she said, not offering assurance but more of her denial. She wouldn't accept any culpability for what her hatred had started, for the deaths she'd caused…maybe even her own great-granddaughter's.

Elena shook her head, disgust churning her stomach along with the fear. She wouldn't let her grandmother off that easily. "You're just as sick as Roarke is."

"I didn't tell him to kill anyone," Thora maintained, the lines pulled tight around her mouth. "I just wanted the charms."

Elena laughed; it rang out with a shrill note as hysteria threatened to overtake her. She drew in a deep breath, summoning the strength she'd never really realized she had. Until now. "You had one of the charms in this house the whole time. But because of how much you hated my mother, how much you hated my Durikken heritage, I hid it from you. I had the star."

"Had?"

"I think Stacia has it now." She prayed she did. The charm might be the only thing keeping her safe…unless Roarke realized she had it. Then her little girl was doomed to the same fate as her ancestors.

The first light of dawn streaked through the windows at the end of the hall, glinting off the plaque on the door proclaiming Roarke Investigations. Joseph closed his hand around the doorknob, but the lock held tight. A few minutes with a maid or a super, and he could either bribe or bully his way inside. But he didn't have time to track down either. So he stepped back, lifted his leg, and kicked. A crack resounded in the hall as the wood jamb splintered. Still the door held tight…until he kicked again.

A quick search of the reception area revealed nothing but old files. So he headed toward the back office and another locked door. He kicked hard enough that it opened on his first attempt.

His hand shaking as anger coursed through him, he fumbled with the lamp on the desk. The shade vibrated, casting eerie green shadows against the wall and across the desk. He dropped into the seat and reached for the drawers. Like everything else, they were locked. Roarke worked hard to keep his secrets.

But not hard enough to keep out Joseph. He reached in his pocket, pulling out the switchblade. Didn't matter if he was wearing ripped jeans or a three-piece suit, he was never without it.

Using the thick blade, he jimmied open the bottom drawer. A book lay inside, the leather cover cracked and worn. He'd never seen anything as old. When he lifted it out, dust or ash dropped from the pages, joining the pieces already covering the blotter on the desk. This was something that Roarke had looked at often. The light picked up a word burned into the cover. The printed letters, embossed with fire, spelled out the name McGregor.

Joseph's gut twisted. Elena was right. Roarke was

the killer. And she'd hired him to find her daughter. She would never forgive herself if something happened to her little girl. She wasn't the only one.

Joseph turned his attention away from the brittle old book; it held only *old* secrets. He wanted to know the new ones; he needed to know where the hell Roarke held Stacia.

He dug back into the drawer, pulling out a pewter trifold frame. Three little girls stared up at him: the youngest with curly dark hair and big brown eyes, the middle one with long red locks and bright turquoise eyes, and the oldest, heart-breakingly beautiful even then, with her pale blond hair and eerie light blue eyes. Stacia was the spitting image of her mother.

He remembered her smile, brighter even than her mother's in the picture Joseph held. Like Elena said, it lit up her eyes, her whole face. And his heart.

"Where are you?" he wondered aloud. And where the hell was Roarke?

In the outer office, something slid. Either a pile of folders, or a chair, alerting Joseph he wasn't alone. But he'd no more than closed his fingers around his switchblade before he heard the cock of a gun and stared up into its barrel.

Chapter 10

"You should have called me. I would have come to you," Ariel said, as she joined Elena on the black leather couch in the living room of the penthouse. "You shouldn't be out by yourself, driving."

"I'm not going to fall apart," Elena insisted. "I can't."

She had to hold it together…for Stacia. And Joseph. Maybe she could stop the killer before her vision of Joseph dying came to pass.

"Elena, you don't always have to be so independent. Let us help you. David's out there right now, trying to find Roarke." And his fiancée's face was pale, her eyes clouded with concern for his safety. "I tried to get a hold of Ty, too. But he's not answering his cell."

"He's focused on Irina," she said. Maybe *she* was with Stacia. Maybe her daughter wasn't alone. Maybe Irina was the woman in the water, being pulled under, catching Stacia when Roarke tossed her in. Elena could never be sure she interpreted the visions correctly.

But even if Irina wasn't with her, Ariel had assured her that Stacia wasn't alone. Their mother was with her, her ghost offering the maternal comfort Elena could not. She glanced around the penthouse, wishing she were like her sister, wishing that she could see ghosts.

"She's not here," Ariel said, her voice soft as she obviously construed her sister's visual search.

Elena bit her lip, holding in the little cry of relief that burned her throat. Then she clarified, "You mean Stacia?"

"Or Mama. Nobody's here but you and me," Ariel said, her eyes narrowing as she studied Elena's face. "So tell me what's going on."

"What do you mean?" She hated keeping things from her sister, from Joseph, but she was good at keeping secrets; she'd kept the truth of her heritage, of her ability, from everyone, even herself, for two decades.

"You're worried," Ariel acknowledged, "but you're not as worried as I thought you'd be."

"Because I haven't fallen apart, you don't think I'm worried?" Nerves ate her alive, churning her stomach, thrashing in her heart and pounding in her head. *God, was she doing the right thing?*

"Something's going on with you," Ariel insisted, "something you're not telling me."

They'd been separated for twenty years. How could her sister know her so well when as adults, they were virtual strangers? But then Joseph had sensed the same thing Ariel did; he'd instinctively known she kept something from him. He'd even managed to pry part of it out of her. But not all of it. Neither would Ariel.

"Did you have another vision?" her sister asked.

Elena held in the little sigh of relief that escaped her lungs. She could share the vision but only the vision. "Yes, of Joseph."

Ariel's turquoise gaze studied Elena. "He's important to you?"

She nodded again, unable to voice her feelings about the man to her sister. Or even herself. But she kept much more from her sister than her feelings.

"What's your vision about?"

"He's dead." Like the others. Like her, if she were the woman in the vat of water.

"Elena…"

She brushed a hand across her face, pushing back her tangled hair. "He promised me he'd stay safe. Joseph isn't the kind of man who makes promises."

"He cares about you," Ariel said.

And because he did, he would put himself in danger. She had to stop him. She reached out, grasping her sister's hand. But before Ariel could entwine their fingers, she ran her fingers down to the redhead's wrist, tugging at the bracelet Ariel wore. "I need your charm."

Ariel's eyes brightened. "You're going to try to force a vision."

She nodded, unable to verbally utter a lie to her sister.

"Of Stacia?" The turquoise eyes dimmed. "Elena, I don't think—"

"You don't think I can handle it? I have to find my daughter," she said. "I have to do *whatever* necessary to get her back."

She hoped Ariel would remember that and understand when she learned the truth, when she realized Elena had lied to her.

Ariel shivered. "But what you're doing—trying to find out her fate—"

"It won't be her fate, not if I can save her, like David saved you." She'd seen Ariel hanging, her head lolling back in the noose, her turquoise eyes

open in the blind stare of death. But David had pre-
vented that from happening. Just like Elena would
prevent any harm befalling her daughter.

Ariel fumbled with the clasp holding her charm
to her bracelet, then pulled it free and dropped the
little pewter sun into Elena's palm. She closed her
fingers over it, holding tight, so that she wouldn't
change her mind. The warmth of the little pewter
sun moved up from her fingertips, dispelling some
of the chill gripping Elena since she'd found
Stacia's teddy bear beneath the bed at a murder
scene. Like Ariel, she was counting on the charms
for salvation, too, more than visions.

But a vision came, heralded by the flash of light
inside her head. An image wavered, beneath the
surface of water. A woman's hair floated up,
darkened with wetness. Her arms flailed, splash-
ing madly beneath the water, sending ripples to the
top so that waves crashed against the sides of the
deep, wooden vat.

Bubbles also rose as the woman fought for
breath beneath the water. The crank, activated by
a remote control, turned, loosening the rope
holding down the woman. Her body shot up, her
head breaking through the surface. Dark blond
hair floated around her pale face, as her eyes stared
up at her killer. Eerie, light blue eyes.

She was the woman in the vat. Not Irina.

Her heart pounded hard as she faced the implication of her vision. She was going to die. She pushed aside the fear. She couldn't worry about herself. Not now.

"Elena? Are you all right?" her sister asked. "Did you just have a vision?"

She shook her head, unable to speak for the fear choking her throat.

"You're worried about Stacia. We'll save her," Ariel said, throwing her arms around Elena and pulling her into a close embrace. "She'll be back with you soon."

Elena squeezed her eyes shut, fighting the tears that threatened. She couldn't fall apart, not now, when she was so close....

She gripped the sun, holding it tightly in her hand as her sister held her. The lightning flashed behind her lids, revealing not just wavering images or snippets of the scene but everything. She saw it all now.

The corrugated metal sides of the building. The catwalk above the vat. And the cement floor below it, where Joseph lay, blood pouring from his chest, pooling around his body as he stared up. His eyes blind in death, he couldn't see what she saw.

The vat where the ropes bound her to the crank, the ripples in the water as Roarke tossed Stacia to her. Then the crank turning, as he tightened the ropes around her ankles, pulling her to the bottom of the deep vat. And as she went under, she pulled Stacia with her. Instead of saving her daughter, she dragged her below the surface…killing her child…her last action before death claimed her, too.

"No…" she murmured. The warmth of the pewter sun offered her no comfort, nor did the tightness of her sister's embrace. She pulled back, shaking.

"What did you see?" Ariel asked, her voice soft with compassion yet vibrating with excitement. "You just had a vision."

She shook her head. "No. N-no-thing," she stammered.

Ariel's brow furrowed as she studied her sister's face. She was not going to accept any more of Elena's lies. "Come on, I know—"

Before she could press any further, the elevator doors swished open in the foyer, and deep voices rumbled. As her vision warned he would try again, Joseph came unknowingly to her rescue. This time it wouldn't kill him.

Ariel ran, heels pounding against the marble floor, and hurled herself into her fiancé's arms. "David, you're all right. I was so worried."

David's arms tightened around her, holding her close to his heart. Ariel's hands patted his back, just above the gun tucked into the waistband of his pants.

"I'm fine," he assured his bride-to-be. "We didn't find the bastard, so we weren't in any danger."

"Just from each other," Joseph muttered, as he walked over to Elena. "You're here. Why didn't you stay at the house?"

"She came for my charm," Ariel answered for her, pulling back from David's possessive embrace. "You're Joseph?"

He nodded. "And you're Ariel." But he didn't spare her sister a glance, all his attention focused on Elena. "You have a charm."

"Can you force a vision?" David asked, his arms still around Ariel's shoulders.

Whenever they were together, the engaged couple always touched, inexplicably drawn together, unable to bear any separation. Elena had never known a love like theirs; she'd never known such a love existed. Until now.

David continued, "We're going to need more to go on in order to track Roarke down."

"It's him?" Ariel asked, needing confirmation. She, of all people, knew Elena sometimes misinterpreted her visions, like when she'd thought David wanted to kill Ariel.

"We found a journal," Joseph said, his green gaze steady on Elena's face, caressing her with his eyes while he kept his hands fisted at his sides.

"A journal?" Ariel asked. "His?"

"It's really old," David answered. "Has McGregor engraved on the cover."

Thora *had* given Eli's journal to Roarke. The old woman had never confirmed Elena's suspicion. Bile rose in Elena's throat as she recalled some of the demented ramblings she read in that journal. She could share this much with them. "It's Eli McGregor's."

"How do you know?" Ariel asked.

Joseph groaned as realization dawned. A muscle twitched in his jaw, beneath the dark growth of stubble clinging to it. "That bitch. Thora had it? She gave it to him. She started all this. Oh, my God…no wonder you couldn't stay there, with her."

"Surely she wouldn't hurt her own granddaughter, her own great-granddaughter?" Ariel asked, horrified.

"You don't know Thora," Joseph said. "Damn her—she started all of this." He whirled and strode toward the elevator, but Elena chased after him.

"Don't," she pleaded. "Don't go to her."

His voice an angry growl, he replied, "But she might know where the bastard is."

That was why Elena didn't want Joseph going to Thora. If anyone could get information out of the old woman, it was Joseph.

"I already talked to her," she said. "Thora never intended this—"

"What the hell did she intend!"

"It all got out of control." She spoke not only of her grandmother's plan but of her own.

"Out of *her* control?" Joseph asked, his eyes wide with doubt.

Would he react the same way when he learned what she'd done, with disbelief and anger? Would he ever look at her as he once had, with desire?

Elena stared at the closed bedroom door as she sat on the edge of the mattress of the four-poster she was supposed to be lying in, trying to rest. She was also supposed to be forcing that vision. But she didn't need to. She already knew what was going to happen...unless she managed to stop it. She couldn't do that here. But she couldn't leave either, not without Joseph or Ariel and David following her.

Proving her point, the door opened. "I didn't want to knock and interrupt," Joseph said, as if to explain his barging in, but she doubted he'd been concerned about her vision.

"You don't believe me," she said, staring up at him. But she didn't see his green eyes bright with life and purpose. She saw them wide with fear, dull with death. Goose bumps raised her skin, as the chill gripped her again, leaving her so cold that all the charms in the world couldn't warm her.

"I believe you," Joseph insisted.

She shook her head. "You don't believe that you'll die—" her breath caught, burning in her lungs as her heart pounded fast and hard with fear "—if you don't back off."

"I believe you," he said again, his green eyes earnest, his darkly shadowed jaw taut with resolve.

Accepting his claim, she nodded. "You just don't care."

He walked closer, then knelt on the floor in front of her. "I care too much. That's why I can't walk away from this, from you."

Elena's heart lurched. Did he share her feelings? How had they gone from adversaries to lovers in such a short time? It wasn't real. Nothing was real. But the vision flashed in her mind again, Joseph lying on the floor. And she knew it was real.

All of it was real.

"You have to," she said, reaching out to run her fingers through his soft, dark hair. "You have to—" she leaned forward, pressing her lips to his. Then she pulled away and finished "—leave me alone."

Joseph caught her chin in his hand, holding her still as his gaze locked on hers, probing. "Something's going on. You're too calm. It's almost as if you're hiding—"

She shook her head, pulling free of his grasp

and rising from the bed. "I can't hide. Not anymore. I know what I am, Joseph. I've accepted that."

A witch, maybe. But first and foremost, a mother who would do anything to save her child. Even sacrifice her own life. But not his. She couldn't let him lay down his life, too.

And she had no doubt that he would. The fear that he'd claimed to not feel in so long, it was in his eyes now, not just in her vision. The green gleamed with fear and suspicion.

"I don't want to leave you alone," he said.

"I'll be fine," she promised him, as she walked toward the door.

"You'll call me? You'll tell me what you see if you have another…"

She nodded. "I'll tell you everything." And she would. Later. If she lived through it.

She'd bought some time for her daughter, some time for herself. Knowing her plan might cost her her life, she wanted to make the best use of those moments. She turned toward the door… and locked it.

Then like Ariel had hurled herself into David's arms, Elena vaulted into Joseph's, knowing he'd catch her. By his own admission, he wasn't the most honorable man. He'd done things of which he obviously wasn't proud. Maybe that was why he was so determined to help her, to redeem himself, to become that white knight he'd sworn he couldn't be for her.

Despite all his warnings about not trusting him, not counting on him, she knew he'd be there. If she let him.

She could only let him for this…for his kiss. For his touch. Reaching up, she delved her fingers into the softness of his dark hair and pulled his mouth down to hers. This could be the last time she felt anything but fear…and maybe regret.

His arms wrapped tight around her, holding her close to his madly pounding heart. The beat of hers echoed his. Frantic. She pushed her tongue through his lips, sliding it over his.

He groaned, then kissed her back with the same desperate passion with which she'd kissed him. His hands slid over her back, pressing her against him until she couldn't draw a breath without breathing him in, the musk and citrus that she'd first smelled in her dreams.

Joseph wasn't a dream. He was real. Alive. And for the moment, so was she.

She pulled his shirt from his pants, then raked her nails up the satin-soft skin of his back. Muscles rippled beneath her touch. He groaned again, then tore his mouth from hers to utter her name. "Elena?"

She answered the question in his voice, in his

green eyes dark with desire, as she tugged him toward the bed. She pushed him down onto the mattress, then stepped back. With trembling fingers she lifted her sweater over her head and let it drop to the floor behind her. Her skirt went next, unclasped and unzipped, so that it pooled at her ankles. She stepped out of the circle of linen and her shoes.

Joseph watched her, his face flushed and intense with desire, even while his eyes still held questions about her change of heart. The green flared, his control snapping, when she reached for his zipper, dragging it down to free his hard erection from the confinement of his pants and then his boxers.

He was the one who pulled off her panties, his hands sliding down her hips and thighs as he pulled the scrap of satin from her. Then he clasped her hips and lifted her onto his lap so that she straddled him.

She lifted, rubbing against his penis, moaning with the intensity of pleasure rippling through her. Then she impaled herself. Their bodies mirrored the frantic beats of their hearts as he drove up and she rode him, meeting every thrust with her hips, welcoming him deeper and deeper into her body and into her heart.

He watched her yet, his eyes intense. His hands

slid up from her hips to tug down the cups of her bra. Her breasts spilled into his palms. As he flicked his thumbs over the hardened nipples, she lost her faint grip on reality and catapulted out of her mind.

Heat coursed through her as her orgasm spilled over him. He gritted his teeth and groaned, then closed his eyes as he pumped into her. His hands slid back to her hips, holding tight, as he poured his desire into her.

He clasped her tight to his chest, where his heart pounded with the same frantic beat. Making love with him hadn't changed anything. It hadn't eased her fear, or his. Maybe he sensed what she knew, that this might be the last time. His lips touched her neck, sliding to where her pulse beat against her skin.

"Elena…"

She pulled free of his embrace, then scrambled back into her clothes. After doing up the last button, she reached for the charm, glinting in the light, where it lay on the bedside table.

"Joseph, I can't explain." Anything. Least of all her feelings for him. She didn't understand them herself. She didn't know why she trusted him when she should trust no man, after her marriage to Kirk. She should trust nobody, after her relationship with her grandmother.

"Elena, what are you trying to tell me?" he asked, his voice thick with concern. "Goodbye?"

"I want you to leave," she said. "I need to be alone." To gather her courage, to do what she had to do…for Stacia's sake and her own.

He struggled. She saw it on his face, in the muscle jumping in his clenched jaw, in the darkness of his green eyes. He wanted to argue with her, to force her to confess the secret he somehow sensed she kept from him. How did he know her better than her husband had after nearly eight years of marriage? She'd let him into her life farther than she'd admitted Kirk, but then, being Joseph, he'd pushed himself in the rest of the way.

But not now. He straightened his clothes and rose from the bed. His jaw set, he nodded, accepting her limitations. This time.

He kissed her again, before he headed out the door. His lips were soft against hers, his breath warm and sweet in her mouth. Even after the door closed behind him, she could taste and feel him.

It would have to be enough.

She opened her palm and stared down at the charm. She didn't need it to force a vision. She'd had enough of those with her star locked away in the table beside her bed. With her other hand she pulled the business card from her pocket, then set it on the bed as she reached for the phone.

The phone barely rang once before he answered

this time, not like last, when she'd contacted him from the phone booth after finding his latest victims. Then it had rung many times until he'd finally answered. And confirmed all her fears. She'd hired to find her daughter the last man she wanted anywhere near her.

The killer.

"What took you so long?" he asked, his voice harsh with impatience. He sounded nothing like the compassionate man who'd met her in his office.

She dragged in a deep breath, bracing herself. "I got it. I have Ariel's charm." Then she swallowed hard, forcing down guilt and fear.

"So you have yours and hers?"

He hadn't found the star. Where had Stacia hidden it? Did she even have it yet?

"Yes," she lied, grateful for her twenty years of practice in lying.

"Bring them to me—"

"Let me talk to Stacia. I want to know my daughter is alive," she insisted.

He sighed. "You talked to her last time."

In the phone booth. Stacia's voice had come softly through the cracked plastic receiver. "I'm okay, Mommy. I'm sorry…"

"Shhhh," Elena had tried to soothe her child while her own heart had beat heavily with fear and dread. "You don't have anything to be sorry about. I love you, honey. I'll—"

He'd pulled the phone away from Stacia before Elena had been able to promise her daughter that she'd get her back. She'd keep her safe.

No matter what she had to do.

"You talked to her a couple hours ago," Roarke said now, no sympathy in his voice.

"You could have…" She couldn't even voice what he might have done to her daughter. Too many gruesome images flashed through her mind…of what he'd done to those other women…

"She's all right. For the moment." How could he be so cruel, so heartless? Because he was just as crazy as Thora. He was a McGregor.

But so was Elena. Maybe that was why she'd concocted her crazy plan. *Mommy's going to save you.* God, she hoped Stacia could read minds, at least hers. It was better if she couldn't read *his.*

"I need proof," she insisted. "I need to talk to my daughter."

"She's fine. She's just not with me right now."

"I can't trust you."

"Well, you're going to have to if you ever want to see your little girl again."

"Alive, Roarke. I want her alive. If she isn't, our deal's off. Two charms for two lives." Stacia's and hers. She'd promised him the charms if he'd let her

and her daughter live. After all, she'd pointed out
to him, she and Stacia were McGregors. He only
wanted to kill Durikkens, like the vendetta war-
ranted. She hoped Thora was right, that he
wouldn't harm them.

He sighed as if his patience wore thin. "I told
you it was a deal."

He was a madman. How could she believe him?

Without hearing Stacia's voice, how could she
trust that her daughter lived? Because she would
appear as a ghost to Ariel if she died, and Ariel
hadn't seen her little niece.

Elena had to believe her daughter was alive,
that Mother was with her, offering her the comfort
Elena longed to give. Or maybe Stacia could hear
Elena's thoughts; maybe she knew her mother was
coming to rescue her.

She swallowed hard, gathering up the courage
she'd found in Joseph's arms. With him, she
became a stronger person. A braver one. "Tell me
where to meet you."

"Alone, Elena," he warned her. "If I see your
shadow, Dolce, he's a dead man."

She knew he spoke the truth with that promise.
She'd already seen what would happen to Joseph
if he tried to play her white knight.

"He doesn't know that I've talked to you. No
one knows." She prayed she wouldn't regret the

decision she'd made, but she saw her bargain with the devil as her best option of keeping alive all of the people she loved.

For them, she would gladly sacrifice her own life.

Chapter 11

Roarke closed his cell phone and slipped it back into his pocket. Satisfaction swelled his chest, and for once the pain in his head abated, the pounding less intense. It was about damned time things went his way.

All the killing and he'd achieved nothing, even though he'd destroyed at least one witch for sure. With her death, he had gained some of her powers, like Eli had all those years ago. Some of her memories had become his, particularly the memory of when she had bestowed the charms on her three daughters. He could also see her ghost although she'd left him alone lately. Maybe she'd finally left this world, resigned to her fate. She couldn't beat him.

Neither could they. Like her memories and her ghost, he also had her ability to see the future. He'd had that before he'd ever found her though. He'd seen the three witches, in those brown robes, circling him. Their red mouths laughing at him as he strained against the stake they'd tied him to... before setting him afire.

He had to kill them. To save himself. He needed the charms for protection. Against the cancer. Against *them*.

Despite all the killing, he hadn't reclaimed a single charm. Until now. Soon he would have two of them. Maybe they would be enough to save him.

He opened the door and stepped into the dimly lit den. The old woman yanked open a drawer and reached inside, as her pale eyes widened with fear.

"You looking for this?" he asked, raising the gun he carried, the gun that had recently killed two people. Regret flashed through him for their lives. They hadn't been witches, but they'd given him no choice. They'd stood between him and what he needed.

And so might *she*.

"Why would you reach for a weapon when you see me?" Donovan Roarke asked, his mouth twitching into a grin. "We're *family,* Thora."

"Wh-when did you take that?" she stammered, her lips pulled so tightly that lines ran in grooves around them like the rays of the little pewter sun. Besides Myra Cooper's memory, he'd seen the charms in a drawing, detailed in Eli's journal, but soon he'd have the sun in his possession. With the star.

And Elena.

"I took the gun when I realized I couldn't trust you," he told her, "that you weren't as dedicated to the vendetta as a true McGregor would be."

Her chin lifted as pride flashed through her fear. "I am a true McGregor."

He shook his head as if disappointed in her. The truth was he hadn't put any faith or trust in her from the beginning. "A McGregor who kept the secret for as long as you did, who ignored the vendetta as long as you did—"

"My son was sick," she said, her voice cracking. "My focus was on him."

As thoughts of his own son, the boy he hadn't seen in so long flitted through his mind, the pain returned with a bite. He winced as it pounded at his skull as if trying to shatter it from the inside out. Maybe once he got the charms, he could spend time with his son again, tell him about his McGregor legacy.

"If you truly cared about your son," he said, "you would have found the charms to save him. You didn't really believe in their powers then or now. You're a fraud, Thora Jones. You're not a McGregor, not any more than your granddaughter or great-granddaughter is."

Her pale blue eyes widened even more. "They are McGregors, too."

"They're Durikken. They're witches. Both of them. They have to die."

His deal with the witch be damned. Because so would he be, if he let them get away. He had to kill them in order to regain his strength.

"No! You can't hurt them!" A tear streaked down Thora's face, but she dashed away the moisture with the back of her trembling hand.

He laughed at her show of weakness. She was definitely *not* a true McGregor. "You're going to tell me you love them? You *love* witches?"

She shook her head. "No. I tried. I just couldn't." More tears glistened in her eerie eyes, but she blinked them back. "But my son loved them. Elijah made me promise to never hurt them."

"He loved Myra Cooper, too. That didn't stop you from trying to hurt her—"

"She was only Durikken, no part McGregor.

They are." Her throat, skin pale and wrinkled, moved as she swallowed hard. "They're all that's left of him. Please don't hurt them, Donovan."

He shook his head and clicked his tongue against the roof of his mouth. The movement, and the slight sound, had him wincing as the pain intensified. "I'm so disappointed in you, Thora. For so long, you were the only one of us who knew about the vendetta."

If she'd found him sooner, if she'd told him about his heritage, about the charms, he might not have gotten as sick as he was. He might have been able to be there more for his own son.

Pushing aside the regrets that ate away at him like acid, he continued, "You let down not just your ancestors but your son. You killed him by not continuing the vendetta, by not reclaiming the charms. *You* killed him."

Her breath audibly caught, then her throat moved again as she swallowed, choking on the remorse and self-loathing reflected in her pale eyes. "That's not true. I loved him. Everything I did I did for him. That's why I found his daughter, why I brought her here even though I hated—"

"You hated Elena. You hated having her here. Then this will make you happy." He glanced at his watch. "In just a little under an hour, you'll be killing her, too, and your great-granddaughter."

She gasped. "No! I don't want them hurt—"

"*Dead,* Thora. They'll be dead, and there'll be *nothing* left of your son anymore."

More tears fell, but she didn't bother wiping them away this time. "I'm not killing anyone—"

He laughed. "You still think your hands are clean? You found me, so that I'd do your killing—"

"No," she insisted, her voice going shrill with denial, "I just wanted you to find the charms."

"And the witches. I was just supposed to let them live once I reclaimed the charms? No, we both know that's not what you wanted. You want them dead. You just don't have the guts, or the power, to do it yourself," he berated her cowardice. "So you're using me."

"That's not what—"

Donovan silenced her by raising the gun, by pointing the barrel at her. "Well, I have the guts to pull the trigger, Thora."

And he did just that, sending the bullet through her head. Blood sprayed across the bookshelf behind her, spattering the safe in which she'd kept Eli McGregor's journal locked away for far too long.

"Soon, very soon," he promised her, staring into her dead eyes. "I'll have all the power…."

He couldn't do what David Koster could, calmly sit and tap on a keyboard. Sure, the guy was doing something by hacking into records and

pulling up everything on the computer that had
anything to do with Donovan Roarke: his phone
bill, his lease agreements, his divorce decree. And
maybe Koster would find some information that
would lead them to the psycho, but not fast enough
for Joseph. And not *physical* enough.

He couldn't sit, especially not now that Koster
had learned that the bodies had been identified.
Warrants had been issued for him and Elena, to
pick them up for questioning in the murders. He
couldn't wait around for the police to track him
down; he had to *do* something.

Koster had understood, muttering something
about Joseph reminding him of his friend Ty, the
cop they hadn't been able to reach. But Joseph
worried that Elena might not understand; that
when she awakened, she'd resent his leaving.

Despite her insistence on being alone, he'd
checked in on her before he left the penthouse.
She'd been sleeping, her chest rising and falling
with unsteady breaths as tears streaked from her
closed eyes. Even in her sleep, she couldn't escape
her fears. Even in his arms, making frantic love
with him, she hadn't escaped them. As he'd held
her, as he'd driven deep inside her, he'd seen the
fear in her eyes, felt it in her body. That was why
she'd made love to him, both times, to escape the
nightmare her life had become.

He understood why she'd used him, and he didn't care. He would do anything to alleviate Elena's fears. But the only thing that would do that forever was bringing Stacia back to her. He had to find her little girl.

Koster's files had given Joseph a starting point for his search. Some of Roarke's leases and the contacts he'd made when he'd formed a cult a few months ago had brought back memories for Joseph. The cult was gone now; David had seen to that. All of the members had been rounded up and questioned, but none had admitted to knowing the identity of the cult leader. Now that they knew his identity, other questions could be asked. And Joseph intended to do the asking. Some of the members hadn't had a real address, just the street.

He pulled his SUV to the curb of one of the streets on the east side of Barrett. This abandoned industrial area housed only empty warehouses and the homeless. He knew these streets well. He'd lived on them for years. In the distance he noted the crooked steeple of an old church, the bell hanging drunkenly in the tower, dangling from only a few ropes.

Roarke had used that church as the headquarters for his cult. Koster had wondered why the killer had used this area, that church. Now that they knew the killer's identity, they'd discovered why. Roarke had been a cop for a short time, and as a rookie, this had been his beat.

Joseph would have been gone then. He'd clawed his way off the streets and back to school, knowing that an education was the only way he'd ever escape this life. Now he opened the door to his truck and stepped back in time, confronting the ghosts of his past for the promise of a future. Elena's and Stacia's. He didn't expect to be part of it; that wasn't why he wanted to find her daughter, to earn Elena's love.

She could never love a guy like him, a guy who had once lived here. He slammed the door and clicked the keyless entry, locking the Lincoln Navigator. Not that locks made much difference down here. He could open a locked vehicle without much problem, like he'd opened Roarke's office and desk. For Elena, he'd been willing to return to his old life.

But his instincts were rusty. He'd been lucky David had been the one to catch him, that it hadn't been Roarke's gun he'd wound up staring down the barrel of because he had no doubt Roarke would have pulled the trigger.

If only he'd found more in the private investigator's office, something to lead him to Stacia. The longer the bastard had her, the less likely the little girl was still alive. Statistically he knew the odds were already more in favor of the kid being dead, especially after what the bastard had done to her other relatives. Maybe it was because he wasn't much of a gambler; he worked too hard for his money to part with it on chance, but he was betting the kid was alive.

His gut twisted with nerves and fear. *She had to be.*

"Son of a bitch," he muttered as he crossed the street and stepped over the garbage and liquor-bottle-strewn gutter to the crumbling sidewalk.

Shadows lurked in alleys and partially boarded-up doorways. Memories of his life, long ago, flashed through his mind. Was that how Elena felt when she had a vision? Helpless? Frustrated? Afraid?

He'd vowed to never feel like that again, but his heart pounded. Not with fear over the past, or his own safety. Fear for the females he cared about, Elena and her daughter. A shadow emerged from a doorway, trailing him. From the corner of his eye, he caught sight of the dark, hulking figure. So he turned into an alley, one he remembered well. Nothing had changed down here; everything was in the same place, as if it had been waiting for him, to suck him back into the dark existence he'd once lived.

He ducked back into another doorway, along

the alley, and waited. When the figure followed, he vaulted from the doorway and threw his arm around the guy's neck, catching him in a stranglehold.

"Shorty, all these years on the street, I figured you'd have gotten smarter," he berated the other man.

"Damn you, Dolce," Shorty cursed him as the six-foot-plus giant struggled in his hold. "You always were a sneaky son of a bitch. You tell me to meet you and you pull this shit!"

"Meet me, not ambush me," Joseph reminded him, releasing his old street buddy before the man broke free. His muscles strained against his suit jacket, hurting with the exertion. He'd gotten soft in the years he'd lived the easy life. Maybe he should have come back sooner, to remember what he'd left.

Shorty stumbled a few feet forward, then swiftly turned, surprisingly fast for a man of his height and girth. Despite being off the streets for a while, Joseph remembered his old friend's signature move and ducked. Shorty's fist slammed into the rotted wood door above his head, breaking it free of its rusted hinges.

No, he never should have come back here. Not sooner. Not now. But he'd had no choice. Too much was at stake, so no risk was too great. Since Shorty had come alone, he didn't want to kill

Joseph. Maybe just hurt him a little, like Joseph leaving the streets and never looking back had probably hurt him.

"Bastard!" Shorty yelled as he flailed his fist around, blood oozing from his knuckles. "You bastard!"

"It's great to see you again, too, Shorty," Joseph said, "But I don't have time for a tearful reunion—"

"Still the same smart-ass—"

"A little kid's life is on the line, Shorty," he interrupted the other man's tirade. "A real sick bastard got a hold of her."

Shorty's face twisted into a grimace. "Oh, God…"

"You know him, Shorty. Donovan Roarke. He used to work this beat."

"Roarke was never no perv," Shorty said. "But he was a mean bastard. Got busted out of the department for excessive force."

"He's crazy, Shorty, and he's got this little kid." He swallowed hard. "She's important. Special." Like her mother. "I gotta know if you've seen him lately."

Shorty shook his head. "Strange shit going on down here. This weird cult took up at the church a while back. The leader roped some of my regulars into it, promising them food and a warm place to stay."

"That was Roarke."

"That prick cop was one of the guys in the brown robes?"

"He was the *leader*." A manipulative son of a bitch who had fooled several people, Elena included.

Would she ever forgive herself? Her face was forever etched in his mind, the tears streaking from her closed eyes as she wept in her sleep; the only time he'd seen her cry, the only time she hadn't been too proud to fight her tears, when she was sleeping. His heart ached with the hurt in hers. He had to help her.

"Have you seen him around lately?"

Shorty studied Joseph for a moment, his dark eyes hard. "I should charge you for this, Dolce. I heard you made it big, but you never brought any of it back to the neighborhood."

Joseph bit the inside of his cheek and fisted his hands, prepared for the other man to launch another attack. "I've never been a user, Shorty."

"I know you don't do drugs, that's how you got outta here." Resentment burned in his old friend's dark eyes. "But you shoulda come back before now."

And helped Shorty out. "I will. If you do the right thing. She's just a little kid…." Whose smile could melt the heart of anyone she met, even of the man who hadn't believed he still had one.

"There's another stranger down here, wearing some stupid disguise, could be Roarke. Might be another psycho. You know this neighborhood, Joe."

"I've been gone a long time," Joseph reminded him. Then swallowing hard, he admitted, "I need your help."

Shorty's chest puffed out with pride as he granted Joseph's favor. "I'll put the word out. I'll find 'em for you."

While Shorty barked orders into his cell, Joseph picked up his untraceable one and dialed Koster. "Find anything else?"

Koster's ragged sigh preceded his warning, "You're not going to like this."

Joseph's heart shifted in his chest as fear painfully gripped it. "Oh, God, he's killed her—"

"No, or at least Ariel doesn't think so." Because she hadn't seen her ghost yet. That was what Koster meant; now Joseph just had to accept that this woman could see ghosts. She was Elena's sister. He had to accept it.

"That's good news then," he said.

"Elena's gone. She left his card on the bed in the guest room. She made a deal, Joe."

Koster didn't need to spell it out. Joseph knew the terms she'd agreed to, probably without a moment's hesitation.

Herself for her daughter.

* * *

The woman's face wavered in and out of focus as the water covered her, sucking her under and stealing the breath from her body.

"Let my mommy go!" Stacia shrieked, tugging at the man who held her, trying to pull free of his hard grasp. Like at the hotel, when he'd dragged her out from under the bed, he tightened his grip, his fingers biting into the muscles of her arms, threatening to snap the delicate bones beneath.

She didn't care if he hurt her. She had to save her mommy. "Let her go!"

Mommy struggled to the surface, her arms breaking through the water first, then her face. She gasped for breath and blinked away water that clung to her lashes, as she stared up at Stacia and the bad man. She reached up, trying to rescue her. That was why she'd come, to save Stacia from the bad man.

But he'd tricked her. He'd tricked them both.

"No," Stacia whimpered, fighting her way free of not just the killer but the grasp of the bad dream. Mommy said that was all they were—bad dreams.

But she was wrong.

The dream of Daddy dying, it had come true. The bad man had killed him and Daddy's friend, just like Stacia had dreamed it. As he'd dragged her from under the bed, she'd seen the blood…on his robe, on the bed and the floor as they'd passed through the room where he'd killed them.

She'd screamed, but no one had heard her. No one had come to help her then. But Mommy was coming. And she would walk right into the bad man's trap.

Stacia tried to scream now, but some dry, scratchy cloth filled her mouth, part of it shoved between her teeth, another part of it wrapped around her head, like the rope that tied her wrists behind her back. The rope was scratchier than the cloth, and when she fought to get free, it cut into her skin. She whimpered again at the pain, which pressed down on her like the fear.

She'd never been so afraid and not just because it was dark. She lay in some small room, on a cold cement floor. Alone for now.

A while ago, noises had drifted under the door. Scraping, like stuff was being moved around. And men's voices, murmuring low. Grunts as they worked hard at whatever they'd been doing in the metal building the bad man had brought her to. Then everything had gotten quiet, and left alone in the silence, she'd fallen asleep.

But the man would be back. That was what she feared, his return and what he'd do then. To her. And Mommy.

Something touched Stacia's cheek, as if to wipe

away the tears streaking down her dirty face. She shivered, hoping it wasn't one of the mice she could hear in the dark, their fingernails scratching against the concrete.

"It's okay, baby," a soft voice murmured.

Stacia opened her eyes to a strange glow. A faint orange light illuminated a dark haired woman who hovered over her. *Grandma.* She'd found her.

So, too, would Mommy. While Stacia wanted to see her mother again, she didn't want the bad man to hurt her, too. Not like he had Daddy and his friend….

More tears flowed from her eyes and choked her throat. Her grandmother's ghost reached for the cloth gagging Stacia, but her wispy fingers passed through the fabric, the same with the ropes at her wrists and ankles.

She couldn't free Stacia, so the little girl struggled anew, fighting the ropes and trying to spit out the gag. But there was no escape. Not from the ropes, not from the little, dark room and not from the bad man.

If only she hadn't lost the charm.

The little metal star would have kept her safe, but it had slipped from her hand when the man had carried her into this cold, dark place. She hoped the bad man didn't find it. She knew what Mommy had told him, that she'd bring him both charms. If he found it, he'd know her mommy had lied to him.

Did it matter, though?

He was going to kill her anyway. Because he had lied, too. He wasn't going to let them go, not even if Mommy could give him both charms.

He was going to kill them. And tied up and gagged, Stacia could do nothing to stop him. The door, to the little room where he'd locked her, creaked open. Only dim light filtered into the room, not as bright as the orange glow surrounding her grandmother's ghost.

But then the man, standing in the doorway, blocked most of the light. He wore a brown robe, like he had at the motel. The hood of it covered his head and most of his face. Only his eyes gleamed in the shadows.

Lying on the cold floor, Stacia shivered and prayed for someone to help her. But no one could hear her thoughts but maybe her grandmother's ghost. She stood between Stacia and the bad man, but he walked right through Grandma Myra's misty body to pick up Stacia.

"Let me show you what I have planned for you and your mother," he said, his voice soft as if he was nice. He had talked to her that way at the hotel, too, and here, when he'd tied her up.

But he didn't fool her. Stacia knew he was a bad man. And she already knew what he had planned for her and her mother.

Death.

Chapter 12

Joseph paced the warehouse, skirting old crates and pieces of rusted metal, chunks of the building that had either come off the sides or fallen off the roof. No wonder Roarke had been drawn to this area—there were a lot of great places to hide. But, despite the warrant issued to bring Joseph in for questioning in the Lancaster Inn murders, he wasn't hiding. He was waiting.

Metal groaned as a sliding door edged open, letting afternoon light steal into the dark shadows of the room. Joseph slipped behind a tall wooden crate, instinctively pulling up the hard-learned invisibility shield he'd used when he was a kid; it was how they'd hidden to avoid rousting police officers and do-gooder social workers. He'd been good at being invisible…until the day he'd sought out one of those social workers, choosing a group home and school over the brutality of the streets.

Shadows ate the light as a group of men entered the warehouse, pushing someone ahead of them. The man fell to his knees on the cement, barely managing to muffle a groan.

"Nobody's here," grumbled a boy not much older than Joseph had been when he'd hit the streets. But the kid was big, and so were the young men with him, in the group of six.

Roarke hadn't stood a chance. If it was Roarke. Although Joseph had only seen the private investigator's picture once, in the grainy driver's license photo Koster had pulled up on the computer, he would never forget what the son of a bitch looked like. The reddish-brown hair, the dark brows, the cold, dead eyes…

"*He's* here," a deeper voice said, as Shorty joined them in the warehouse. "Son of a bitch could always make himself invisible."

"Helps when someone's trying to smash in my face," Joseph reminded him, as he stepped from behind the crate. He wasn't entirely sure he could trust Shorty yet. If Shorty had been the one to get out and not him, he knew he would have been filled with resentment, too.

"We found 'em," Shorty said, as if to prove his trustworthiness.

Joseph had to step closer to see about that. The man knelt on the floor yet, one of his legs stiff in the cast showing through the rips in his old jeans. Koster had bragged that Ariel, during their last brush with the killer, had gotten a bullet in the guy. Had she hit his leg? The guy's head was bent, his face shadowed from Joseph's view.

"What about the girl?" he asked the kids. "Did you see him with a little girl?"

One of the kids looked to Shorty first, then shook his head. "No. He's always alone."

"But asking about some girl," another kid chimed in, then glanced to Shorty as if fearful he'd spoken out of turn.

Joseph's heart kicked. Maybe she'd gotten away. "A little blond girl?"

"No. A girl in her twenties, dark hair…"

Joseph recalled the trifold frame he'd found in Roarke's desk. The faces of the three girls, the littlest one with dark hair and big brown eyes. Irina.

Joseph reached out to grab the guy's hair to jerk up his head, but the man sprang to his feet and slammed into Joseph, knocking him back and into the crate. The wood splintered beneath their weight, dropping them both to the cement floor. Joseph rolled and raised his fist, ready to pummel the guy. Then he noted the eyes, dark blue, intense but not crazy or dead. "You're not Roarke."

The guy's fist stopped just short of Joseph's mouth as he paused and asked, "Who the hell's Roarke?"

Joseph studied the guy lying on the cement floor. His marine-cut dark hair was at odds with the old coat and worn jeans he wore. "Who are you?"

A muscle twitched in the guy's jaw as he studied Joseph in return, no doubt debating what to tell him. Fact or fiction.

"Come on, buddy," he prodded, raising his fist again. "I don't have time to waste. A little girl's been abducted."

The blue eyes narrowed, a scarred brow lifting. "A little girl? Who?"

"Tell me your name—"

A muscle ticked in the guy's jaw, dread thickening his already raspy voice when he said, "Not Stacia Phillips…"

Joseph eased back, vaulted to his feet, then dragged up the guy. His hands clenching in the collar of the old wool coat, he shook him. "Tell me who the hell you are, or I'll pound it out of you—"

The guy pitched his voice low, his words

intended only for Joseph's ears. "I'm a cop." The muscle twitched again. "I *was* a cop."

"So was Roarke. That doesn't make me trust you any more. How do you know Stacia?"

"Call David Koster—"

"Shit!" Realization dawned. "You're Ty, the guy nobody could get ahold of today." Now he knew why; the cop had gone undercover.

"So's he your guy?" Shorty asked, his brow puckered as he tried to understand their half-whispered exchange.

"Damn it, no!" He released Ty with such force the guy stumbled back a few steps, then Joseph whirled toward the other members of Shorty's little gang of thieves and drug dealers. "I need your help—"

"First one was free," Shorty interrupted. "The next will cost you."

"Not a child's life. Come on. This sick bastard has her. The guy who ran the cult out of the church. Has anyone seen *him* again?"

When they held their silence, he reached for his wallet. Some muffled sound slipped through Ty's lips, probably surprise that Joseph still had it on him. He opened the leather bi-fold and pulled out all the bills inside, holding them up. "It's yours. I don't give a shit about the money. I have to find that little girl before he kills her. He'll be doing it in some twisted way."

Bile rose in Joseph's throat, choking him as his heart hammered against his ribs. "Torturing her. Come on, do any of you want to see a four-year-old girl tortured?"

The kid who'd spoken first, the youngest one, blinked hard as if fighting tears. He looked to Shorty, who plucked the money from Joseph's hand, then nodded.

"That guy, the one who started that cult thing," the kid said, his voice cracking with either hormones or fear, "he paid a few of us to help him with something."

Ty stiffened beside Joseph. But Joseph reached back, jabbing a finger in the cop's ribs so he would maintain his silence. Joseph had to ask the questions. Because he'd been one of them, and because it was his money, they would only answer to him. He knew the laws of this jungle. "Did you see the little girl?"

The kid shook his head. "No. We helped him move this big barrel."

One of the other kids snorted. "Hell, man, that was bigger than a barrel."

Another chimed in. "It's bigger than the public swimming pool."

Joseph's heart lurched, and he heard the catch of Ty's breath. Drowning. The sick son of a bitch hadn't done that yet, but it was a traditional ritualistic way of killing witches. "Did you fill this barrel with water?"

The kid nodded. "Yeah, after he had us set it up by a catwalk, we filled it with water from the old fire hydrant. The barrel's got some crank and rope in the bottom, too. He can operate it with a remote control. We couldn't figure what he wanted it for…" The kid's face paled, and his eyes widened. "Oh, my God."

"Yeah." Joseph's guts knotted with fear. "Show us where he set this up!"

He had to get there before Elena offered herself as trade. Because he knew Roarke was too crazy to honor any bargain made with a "witch." He intended to kill both mother and daughter. He was going to drown them.

Elena pulled the hood over her hair, just as Roarke had directed, and stepped out of her car. She'd found the brown robe in David's den; he'd infiltrated the cult a month ago, trying to find out the killer's identity. As well as the robe, she'd borrowed some of Ariel's clothes, pulling on jeans, socks and tennis shoes with her sweater. Then she'd used the service elevator to sneak out of the penthouse, to where she'd left her car in the parking garage.

She'd nearly been caught, not by Ariel or David

but the police officers who'd been in the lobby, waiting for David to let them up. She would deal with their questions later, if she made it through her meeting with Roarke.

Or this neighborhood. She'd been down here before though, to this area devastated by poverty, abandoned by businesses who'd moved to more favorable economic quarters. Probably in other countries. Shadows lurked in doorways and alleys. And although she really couldn't see anybody, she felt them watching her as she left her car at the curb and walked down the crumbling sidewalk.

The wind picked up, and the ropes in the steeple creaked in protest as the bell swayed just enough to utter a weak clang. A warning bell? If so, Elena ignored it. She was too close now, too close to where he held her daughter.

Wearing the brown robe would secure her safety in this dangerous area, Roarke had assured her. What would guarantee her safety from him?

She had left the business card for Ariel, knowing her sister would find it soon after she'd left the penthouse. Ariel was too compassionate, too worried about her, not to have checked on her soon.

Koster could trace her cell phone. He had some program where they could track down its location and *his;* they would find the private investigator.

But storming Roarke's fortress now, with sirens and manpower, would risk Stacia's life. Elena had to get her daughter away from him first, before the others could try to take Roarke.

He wouldn't surrender without a fight. He was too crazy. And too clever.

But so was she. And she had something even more powerful: her gift. Not a curse. She finally accepted her ability for what it was. But her ability paled in comparison to her daughter's multiple gifts. She was relying on those, more than her own, to save their lives.

Her acceptance was new, her risk too great, for her not to have nerves clenching her stomach and dampening her palms. She drew a deep breath and walked toward the warehouse Roarke had indicated. As he'd said, the shadow of the church's steeple lay across its rusted metal roof.

And inside, probably bound and gagged, lay her daughter. He better not have harmed Stacia. Elena's arms ached to hold her baby, to comfort her and ease the fear the poor child had to be feeling. If she were still able to feel...

She hoped Ariel was right, that Mother was with Stacia, offering the comfort Elena longed to give her. Soon she'd be able to comfort Stacia herself.

She passed under the shadow of the church,

then glanced down the side of the warehouse, looking for the hole in the metal side he had described to her. She'd just entered the narrow path between buildings when a big hand closed over her mouth and a strong arm wound around her waist, lifting her off her feet.

She kicked out, but the long robe tangled around her legs and the rolled-up cuffs of Ariel's too-long jeans, trapping her as his arm trapped hers at her sides. He carried her through that opening he'd described, jagged metal catching at the robe. A rusted piece tore his skin, sending a long, red gash down his arm. As he flinched in pain, his hold loosened.

Elena bit at his hand, sinking her teeth into his palm. He dropped her onto the cement, her hip hitting the hard surface. She held in a cry of pain, and a scream for help as he trained a gun barrel between her eyes.

"You're not going to shoot me," she said, striving for calmness and managing to infuse her voice with icy imperiousness. She needed to remind him she wasn't just Durikken/Cooper. "I'm a McGregor. And so is Stacia."

That was the main reason she'd come alone, figuring the heritage she had always hated might actually prove her salvation. Thora had to be right; he wouldn't kill one of his own. As dedicated as he was to carrying out the McGregor legacy, he wouldn't harm a McGregor.

His mouth lifted into a reluctant grin. "So I'll *spare* you? You think that's going to work?"

Not only had she thought that, she'd counted on it, for her safety and Stacia's.

He laughed. "I just killed Thora. She was much more McGregor than you'll ever be."

Regret, not pain, flashed through her as she noted the drops of blood on the barrel of the gun. Some were Kirk's. And his friend's. And Thora's. So much blood spilled for vengeance. "This wasn't what she wanted…."

"The killing?" Roarke shook his head. "Except for her own, I think it's exactly what she intended. Even yours and your daughter's. You're witches."

She had no protest, not now. She'd finally stopped denying who and what she was…even though it was probably going to cost her life.

He shook his head, as if pitying her. "I can't let you live."

Now her heart lurched, hurting her ribs it knocked so hard against them. "Stacia—you haven't—"

"She's alive…but ready to die. She *knows*." Despite his intentions, his voice held awe and respect for her child. "Is that her gift? Is she psychic?"

Elena nodded. "Like me."

"And your mother." He glanced around, his dark eyes wild, as if he could see Myra Cooper's ghost, too.

"Because of that, we know what's coming." She gestured toward the tall, round vat in the middle of the warehouse. Water pooled around it, leaking through the cracks in the wood. "I saw that already."

"And still you came," he said, his brow furrowing as if she intrigued him.

"She's my daughter," she said, knowing that would explain it all; that any parent would understand. "What would you do for your son?"

He clenched his jaw and spoke through gritted teeth, "Kill."

She nodded again, then noted how his grip on the gun tightened. A jagged, purple vein throbbed at his temple. With pain or fear? She wasn't going to kill him; she didn't have that kind of ability.

But she would die for her child. Just not *with* her child. That wasn't the plan.

Despite the shadows in the warehouse, light flashed with an image through her mind. Joseph lying on this dirty cement floor, blood pooling around him like the water around the vat. Pouring from his wounds, as he stared up at her...in fear.

Like Joseph would have died for her...if she would have let him.

Although she remained on the floor, amid the

dirt, debris and ever encroaching water, she lifted her chin with pride and demanded, "I want to see my daughter."

His mouth lifted again as if she amused him. "You will. Soon," he said, with more threat than promise.

Another image flashed through her mind. Him, dropping Stacia into the water with her, letting her arms do to Stacia what the rope around her ankles did to her, pull her under, drown her.

"Now!" she insisted.

He laughed again. "Oh, it's really too bad that you're a witch. I can see the McGregor in you... even more than in your grandmother."

Comparing her to Thora was no compliment, no matter how he'd intended it. Thora had started up the witch hunt again; she'd found this distant relative and begun the nightmare that had already cost so many lives. How many more would die in the name of vengeance?

He shook his head, as if regretful. "But still...I can't let you live."

"You have to," she insisted. "Or you'll never get the charms."

His shout shook his body and nearly rattled the metal walls of the warehouse. "You brought them!"

She spoke calmly, as if his voice didn't ring in her ears. "No."

"You lying bitch!" he said, striking her with his hand across her face.

She tasted blood, metallic and bitter, as it leaked from her split lip into her mouth. "You'll get the charms…when you let my daughter go."

He shook his head and retrained the bloody barrel of the gun on her face. "No, I'll kill you both now."

"And *nobody* will ever see the sun and star again," she threatened.

He reached down, pushing aside the hood to tangle his hand in her hair and drag her to her feet. "We're going to get the charms now."

She breathed a little sigh of relief that he believed her, that he didn't search her instead. In the pocket of the jeans she'd borrowed from Ariel, she'd hidden the little sun in the lining at the bottom. Perhaps the charm was too small for him to feel through the denim, even if he searched her, but its warmth pressed against her leg, boosting the courage she fought to keep from slipping away.

"If I give you the charms now, you'll kill us," she said. "I'm not going to let you do that."

His hand tightened in her hair, bringing tears of pain to her eyes. But she blinked them back. She couldn't afford to show any weakness; a man like him preyed on weakness, like Thora's insanity.

"You're not the one giving the orders," he told

her, his voice hard with anger and frustration. "Thora learned the hard way that neither was she."

"Thora didn't have what you want, but I do," she reminded him.

He shook her. His voice vibrating with rage, he screamed at her, "Where are they!"

"Let my daughter go, and I'll tell you." Where one of them was. Only Stacia knew where the other was. But at least he didn't. He hadn't found the pewter star on the little girl.

Maybe he didn't have her; maybe her child had gotten away from him…and Elena had walked right into a trap.

"Mommy…" a soft voice called out.

Elena glanced around, trying to find her child inside the vast warehouse. Besides the leaking barrel, other crates filled the metal building. The wooden boxes, of all shapes and sizes, wound across the cement as if set up in a haphazard maze. Other debris was strewn around them. Her child could be anywhere.

"Mommy," Stacia called again, her voice coming from above, as if she were an angel calling down from heaven.

Her heart pounding with fear and dread that maybe she could hear ghosts now, Elena looked up. Her daughter wasn't an angel, but that realization brought her no relief.

At the edge of the catwalk, above the vat filled
with water, stood Stacia, inches from falling into
the depths of the barrel. She must have worked off
the gag that hung now around her neck, like a bedraggled cloth noose. Her arms were at odd angles,
bound behind her back, as her ankles were bound
together. If she fell in, she wouldn't be able to
swim the strokes Elena had taught her last
summer.

If she fell in, she'd drown…like the witch Roarke
called her. As Elena watched her, horrified by the
danger her baby was in, Roarke rapped his gun
against the ladder leading up to the catwalk. The
narrow metal platform shuddered from the force of
his blow, and Stacia swayed on the edge of it.

"No!" Elena shouted, clutching at his arm.
"Don't hurt her!"

"Tell me where the charms are. Now!" He lifted
the gun, rapping it again against the ladder,
sending the catwalk into another buckle beneath
Stacia's bound feet.

Fear coursed through her, and some of Elena's
old inclination for denial returned. She almost
closed her eyes, but she fought against the instinct.
If she did, she might never see her daughter again.

Chapter 13

"This is it?" Joseph whispered as he followed Shorty's gesture toward the abandoned warehouse.

"That's what my boys say, it's true," he said, as if offended.

Joseph nodded. "If you're right, if the little girl's in there, there'll be more money, Shorty."

"Let's not talk money now," Ty grunted in disgust. "Let's call the police."

Joseph's heart lurched as he noted the silver Lexus parked at the curb just past the church. "There's no time. Elena's in there. We need backup. Now."

Ty's raspy voice lowered. "We're going to use a bunch of thugs?"

Joseph shook his head. "No, you're all going to wait out here. I'm going in alone. I don't want to spook this crazy bastard any more—"

"Who's the crazy one," Ty muttered.

"Let me play this my way first." He might have sounded confident to the other men, but inside he quavered with nerves and that damned fear he hadn't felt in so long. But it wasn't fear for himself, for putting his life at risk by going in alone; his fear was all for Stacia and Elena.

"Trust him," Shorty told the cop. "Joe knows how to go invisible."

Ty studied him, his gaze going over Joseph's tailored dress pants and shirt. "You lived down here."

Joseph nodded. "I can slip in there without him knowing it."

Until it was too late for Roarke to harm anyone else. He shoved his hand in his pocket, closing it around the smooth handle of his switchblade. "You guys wait outside, guard all the exits, so the son of a bitch can't get away this time."

Not that Joseph intended to let him get away, or to live, especially not if he'd harmed either the little girl or the woman Joseph loved.

The cop jerked his chin, agreeing to his

kamikaze plan. With the lives of a child and a woman at stake, no risk was too great.

Certainly not for Joseph. Gliding with the silent steps he'd perfected in his youth, he moved between the buildings, keeping to the shadows. Crouched low, he caught the glint of something metal in the weeds growing against the side of the warehouse.

When he reached down, the dull point of a little pewter star pressed into his finger. The charm. The one Elena had looked for back at the hotel when she'd found the teddy bear under the bed. But she hadn't found this. Stacia had kept it with her. Until now.

The little girl had been here. She'd dropped this, either so others could find her, or so that Roarke wouldn't find it. When Joseph palmed the charm, the metal warmed his skin. If he hadn't believed before, he would have realized then that there was something magical about the charms…and about the women who possessed them.

Through a coarse opening in the side of the warehouse, the metal pulled back like the lid of sardine can, he caught sight of Elena, standing proud and strong before Roarke. Her chin lifted, her blue eyes icy, she stared down the deranged killer. "Let Stacia go," she demanded in that imperious voice of hers. "*She* can retrieve the charms."

"And if she doesn't come back…"

"You still have me." Her deal was nonnegotiable, her life for her daughter's. Even while fear pounded in Joseph's heart, it also swelled with pride and love.

Damn, she was something.

Roarke shook his head. "Not good enough."

"You want the charms," Elena maintained. She lifted her head, staring up at her daughter posed at the edge of the barrel.

Water pooled around the wooden vat, leaking from between the slats. The child swayed on the metal platform, just inches above the surface. Her blond hair lay in tangled curls against her head. Her pajamas were stained with dirt and something else, maybe blood. Her hands and feet were bound. What kind of sick bastard would put a child through all this?

A crazy one.

Joseph's fingers tightened around the switchblade. He had to get to Roarke. But the man held a gun, its barrel close to Elena's head. If he caught sight of Joseph, he'd forget his rituals and pull the trigger.

"I'll bring her down here," Elena said, as if their argument was settled, as if she'd won.

She didn't realize her pride and guts couldn't beat a man with a gun. Joseph's own guts twisted. If Roarke got them both onto the catwalk above the vat of water, he wouldn't let the opportunity pass…not even for the charms.

As they both turned toward the catwalk, he slipped into the opening behind them, shrinking into the shadows along the wall. Despite his invisibility, someone spotted him. He just caught the soft gasp that slipped through Stacia's lips.

Oh, sweetie, don't give me up. Our secret. Our little secret. He tried beseeching her with his gaze, but from the distance, she wouldn't be able to read his eyes any easier than his mind.

She turned though, staring down at her mom and Roarke. The kid was already afraid of the dark; heights and water would probably be added to that list now. She'd been through so much. He had to get her out, had to get her to safety before she fell into that barrel of water and drowned just like Donovan Roarke intended.

Sticking close to the corrugated metal wall, he circled around back of the vat, out of Roarke's line of vision. But not Stacia's. She turned toward him, not conspicuously but just cnough to cast furtive glances his way. For four years old, she was damned smart. Hell, she was smarter than some of the adults he knew; at the moment, himself included.

Going in by himself might not have been the best plan. But if the others had come with him, and

Roarke had heard them, he would have pulled the trigger already, killing both Elena and Stacia.

His heart clenched with fear and dread, Joseph waited, not entirely sure of his next step, as he listened to the argument on the other side of the vat.

Elena implored the madman, "Let me get her down from there before she falls into the water. You'll never get the charms then."

"You know," he said, his voice thick with amusement in his sick plan, "I was going to put you in the barrel first—"

"I know," Elena said.

And Joseph realized she'd had a vision about all of this. She'd seen her own murder as well as his.

God, he'd promised her he wouldn't get killed. He *never* made promises. Now he remembered why: they were pretty much impossible for him to keep.

Metal clanged against metal, then the catwalk rattled. Elena gasped. So did Stacia as the metal shifted beneath her feet. She stood so close to the edge of the water-filled vat, her ankles bound together and her hands tied behind her back. If Roarke shook the catwalk just a little more, she'd fall into the water and be helpless to save herself.

"No!" Elena shrieked.

Joseph couldn't see them, but he heard the

crack of a slap and the cry that slipped from Elena's lips. She'd tried to fight him, but no one could match a madman for strength.

Or manipulation. "I'll tie her to the shaft I was going to tie you to. I'll drag her under the water. Then let her up just as she's about to drown. Only to do it over again and again...unless you bring me the charms...."

And after she did that, he'd kill Elena, too. She couldn't trust him. Why had she ever agreed to meet the madman on her own?

Because she didn't trust Joseph. That had to have been why she hadn't asked for his help. Sure, she'd been worried about her vision, but he could take care of himself. And if she'd given him the chance, he could have taken care of her.

His heart clenched, but he pushed aside the pain that reminded him why he'd never let himself care before. It hurt. But he had his chance now, to save her and her daughter.

He turned his attention to Stacia, teetering on the edge of the catwalk. If she shifted, just a little, she could miss the barrel if she fell...

As if she read his mind, she moved, taking a tiny side step. Then another and another until she stood directly above him on the other side of the vat.

"Hey!" Roarke shouted at her. "I told you not to move! I'll kill your mother right now!"

"Stacia!" Elena called out, as the little girl continued to move down the metal platform. Her mother couldn't see Joseph beckoning to her. She would only see her daughter lean forward and drop off the thirty-foot-high catwalk.

Joseph was as surprised by the little girl's move as Roarke and Elena. *She* trusted him. He wouldn't let her down. He reached out, catching her hurtling body in his arms and pulling her close to his furiously pounding heart.

"Stacia!" Elena's screams rent the air, drowning Roarke's curses, until he slapped her again. Because she didn't run around the barrel to find her daughter, Roarke must have held her.

Now Joseph needed to figure out how to save *her.*

Cradling Stacia with one arm, Joseph reached for his switchblade, hacking the knife through the bindings that had abraded her skin, leaving red marks around her wrists. His gut twisted at the pain and fear she must have endured. Her arms freed, Stacia wrapped them tight around his neck, snuggling close, then whispered in his ear, "You found the charm."

She must have seen it when he'd held out his arms to catch her. No, he'd shoved it in his pocket then, with his switchblade. How did she know?

Like her mom and aunt, the kid had gifts. Maybe more than her mom and aunt.

"You're going to be okay," he whispered back, as the little girl trembled against him.

"Mommy…"

Was living a parent's worst nightmare, thinking her daughter had leapt to her death. His heart ached with her pain. He wanted to soothe her.

"Someone's in here!" Roarke shouted. He must have heard Stacia's murmur.

Shots rang out, the barrel splintering as bullets ripped through it. Water poured through the widening cracks, drenching Joseph and Stacia. He caught the little girl close and ran just as the vat collapsed and water deluged the warehouse.

With nothing to block Roarke's shots, the bullets whizzed close to Joseph. He hunched over the little girl in his arms, trying to protect her as he ran for their lives.

Elena saw her vision clearly now, the bullets ripping into Joseph's flesh, riddling his body. "No!" She wouldn't let it come to pass. As she'd fought her daughter's fate and hers, she would fight for Joseph.

Moments ago Roarke's fist had knocked her to the ground; she sprawled on the cement, the escaped water swirling around her, drenching the robe. As she pulled herself up, the weight of the water-saturated garment pulled at her. She fought for strength, both physical and mental.

For a weapon, she grabbed up a piece of the vat, a long, water-logged board. Muscles straining, she raised the board above her head.

Roarke must have sensed her movement, or caught it out of the corner of his eye, because he turned back just as she swung. His eyes widened in shock and surprise as the board connected with his head. The gun dropped from his hand. Water splashed as it clattered to the cement. Then his body joined the gun as he crumpled.

She whirled away from him, running in the direction Joseph had gone with Stacia in his arms. He'd rescued her daughter. Those horrifying moments when Stacia had fallen from the shaky metal platform flashed through her mind again. The barrel obscuring her vision, she'd been left to imagine her daughter's fragile little body breaking against the cement floor.

But Joseph had caught her.

Elena's heart pounded with fear and dread. Would she find him, as she had in her vision, lying on the floor, bleeding to death?

She wound through the maze of crates and debris, trying to find him. What she discovered had her pulse racing, her lungs laboring for breath. Blood spattered the wooden crates, and droplets peppered the dirt-covered floor.

One of Roarke's shots had hit him, just as she'd

feared. She opened her mouth to scream his name, but before she could utter anything, a hand clamped hard over her face. Unlike when Roarke had grabbed her, she felt no fear, only heat and relief as her back was pressed against a hard chest, to the heart that beat hard and heavy, matching the frantic rhythm of hers. Strong arms closed around her.

She breathed deep, dragging in the mingled scent of citrus and musk.

Joseph…

He leaned close to her ear, his breath hot as he whispered, "Where is he?"

"I hit him with a board. He's down—"

His arm tightened a moment, as if he embraced her. Then he slipped away. Before she could follow him, a small hand gripped her robe. "Mommy…"

Elena scooped up her daughter, holding her close to her heart as love and relief poured through her. "Honey, are you all right?"

The little girl nodded as her pale eyes shimmered with unshed tears. She was being so strong. So brave. At only four years old.

Tears burned Elena's eyes and throat. She clutched Stacia close, so grateful just to hold her baby again. "I love you so much…."

"Mommy, Joseph's hurt. He's bleeding."

He'd kept her back to him, so she hadn't seen him before he'd slipped away. What if Roarke wasn't unconscious? What if he hurt Joseph more? What if he'd reclaimed his gun?

She should have grabbed it when it had fallen. She should have shot the man who'd killed her mother and aunts, who'd threatened her daughter's life.

Arms aching to hold her, she forced herself to release Stacia. "Stay here, honey. I have to see if he's okay."

She'd barely stepped back into the maze of crates before she heard his voice, raised in anger. "What the hell—"

A big black man stood near him, in the water pooled on the floor amid the strewn bits of wood…and the gun. "He can go invisible, too, Joe. He's gone. The boys and that Ty guy are looking for him."

A small hand slipped into Elena's, Stacia as unwilling to be separated from her mother as Elena was to have her daughter separated from her. "He got away, Mommy…."

"We'll be okay," she assured the little girl as they joined Joseph in the water.

With her free hand, she touched his head, where blood ran from a cut near his temple, streaking over his dirt-smeared cheek and running off his darkly stubbled jaw to soak his shirt. "Are you okay?"

He nodded, his green eyes hard with anger…

and that fear he'd sworn he couldn't feel anymore. "The son of a—" With a glance at Stacia, he cut himself off. "He got away."

"I hit him hard," Elena insisted. She'd seen him crumple to the ground. How had he recovered so quickly? He was not an ordinary man, which made him far more dangerous than she'd even realized. She should have shot, should have killed him when she'd had the chance. But then she would really be more McGregor than Durikken.

She'd rather be a witch than a killer.

Stacia snuggled against her. "It's okay, Mommy. He can't hurt us. We have the charm. That's why the bullets missed Joseph. He had it."

Joseph reached in his pocket and pulled out the charm, as if just remembering that he had it. In his palm the little pewter star glinted in the last light of the day streaming through the crude opening in the side of the warehouse. Along with the light, sound filtered in, sirens whining in the distance.

His friend clasped Joseph's shoulder. "You're as crazy as I remember. But now I see why." He nodded at Elena and Stacia before slipping through the opening in the wall and disappearing into the shadows.

"Who was he?" Elena asked.

Joseph shrugged. "Someone I trusted to help."

Along with the fear and frustration, hurt darkened his green eyes.

Regret pulled at Elena. "Joseph…"

"You didn't have to do this alone. You could have trusted *me*."

Before she could explain her reasons for acting alone, people invaded the warehouse. Police officers, paramedics, David and Ariel, as well as a familiar-looking dark-haired man in torn jeans and an old coat; he had to be David's friend, Ty, looking more like vagrant than lawman.

"How'd you let him get away!" Joseph berated Ty.

The other man shook his head, his dark blue eyes filling with self-disgust.

"The son of—" David noted Stacia's presence and cut off his curse like Joseph had. "He's slippery, Joe."

Paramedics moved around them. "Please check his head," Elena beseeched them, pointing toward Joseph's wound.

He shrugged off the assistance of a man in a white shirt. "I'm fine. Really. Check the little girl. She's hurt."

As one of the paramedics reached for her, Stacia burrowed deeper in her mother's arms. "I'm okay," she murmured into Elena's neck.

"She should be checked out," Ariel said, meeting her sister's gaze over the little girl's head. Her turquoise eyes revealed a mixture of relief and hurt.

Her arms aching with the effort, Elena released her daughter to the young female paramedic reaching for her. "It's okay, sweetie," she assured her daughter. "Mommy's right here." And never intended to be separated from her again.

As the paramedic checked out Stacia's wrists and ankles, where red scratches marred her pale skin, Elena turned back to her sister.

"I'm sorry," she whispered, regretting her lies. She'd hurt Joseph and Ariel.

The redhead nodded. "You were trying to save your daughter. I understand."

At least one of them did. Joseph kept his back to her as he talked low with Ty, David and the police officers who'd come in with the paramedics. She only caught his "no" as again he refused medical treatment.

"You're Mr. Joseph Dolce?" one of the officers asked him.

He nodded, and as he did, the officer pulled his arms behind his back and locked handcuffs around his wrists.

"You're under arrest for suspicion of the murders of Kirk Phillips and Felicia Hanover."

"No!" Elena shouted.

"No!" Stacia echoed her protest. "It wasn't him. It was the bad man."

The other officer turned to Elena. "And you're Mrs. Elena Jones-Phillips?" he asked.

Before she could even nod, cold metal closed around her skin, locking her wrists together. Not only had Donovan Roarke escaped, she and Joseph were being arrested for his crimes.

Chapter 14

"Where's Joseph?" Elena asked her future brother-in-law as he held open the door to the police department.

While she'd been subjected to hours of questioning in the murders of her husband, her mistress and her grandmother, David had worked behind the scenes to secure her release.

"Did you get him cleared of all the charges, too?" she asked hopefully as she followed him down the cement stairs leading from the police station to the street.

"You're not exactly cleared," David said. "Not yet. Not until you let the authorities talk to Stacia."

She shook her head. "I don't want her reliving everything she's gone through."

Thankfully her child was safe with her aunt and the security team David had guarding the penthouse. Ariel had pulled strings to get Stacia released into her custody instead of child protective services. After the system had failed her more than once, her sister had a deep aversion to child protective services, but she also had a social worker who owed her a favor.

"The police need to talk to Stacia as a potential witness," David reminded her. The only reason the police hadn't taken Stacia into protective custody had been Ariel's insistence that the child be taken to the hospital and checked out.

"She didn't see anything. She was hiding under the bed when Kirk and Felicia were murdered." That was what she'd had Ariel tell the social worker, too.

"She might not have seen him pull the trigger, but she knows Roarke killed them and then kidnapped her. Stacia is the only one who can corroborate your story," David insisted, ever logical.

"Joseph and I have alibis for when Kirk and Felicia were murdered—"

"Having each other as alibis doesn't exactly help your case," David said.

Joseph had told her the same thing.

"Can you get him out?" Her stomach clenched with dread over the thought of Joseph spending the night in jail. He'd already revisited his past to help her and her daughter. She couldn't force him to do it again.

"Elena—"

She shuddered. "Oh, God, to get him released, if the police have to talk to Stacia—"

"No!" a deep male voice protested.

Elena whirled back toward the police department. Joseph stood just outside the circle of light from the street lamp, forever a man living in the shadows. Not like Donovan Roarke had. These shadows weren't of evil; these shadows were of Joseph's past that he never seemed quite able to shake off no matter how far he was removed from the life he'd once lived.

"Nobody's going to put that little girl through anything else," Joseph said, "especially not for me."

Elena's heart lurched, and for the first time she realized the depth of her love for Joseph Dolce. Fathomless. At first she'd hated and mistrusted him, then she'd desired and cared, but now, she was truly, deeply in love, and he wouldn't even meet her gaze because she'd hurt him.

She turned toward David, who silently studied them both. "I'll bring Stacia down to the station in the morning," she told him.

"Or they can send a detective to the penthouse to take her statement. I'll talk to Ty," David promised. "I'm sure he knows which one is the best in dealing with kids. And Ariel'll have Margaret, the social worker, come, too."

Joseph stepped out of the shadows and grabbed David's arm. "Didn't you hear me? I said no."

David expelled a sigh of exasperation and exhaustion. Dark circles rimmed his brown eyes. "The police *have* to talk to her."

"She's just a little kid. She shouldn't have to be put through anything else," Joseph insisted.

Elena's heart melted more, over his concern for her daughter.

"That's not your decision to make," David said. "Even if Elena refuses to have her talk to them, they can subpoena her to testify before a grand jury."

"I'm not refusing," Elena said. "I want them to talk to her." To clear Joseph; she wasn't worried about herself.

When his green gaze turned on her, Elena swallowed hard. Despite swaying on his feet with weariness, his eyes were hard with anger and frustration. Streaks of blood ran from under the white bandage at his temple, down the side of his face to the collar of his shirt, stained red.

Back at the warehouse, she'd ignored the officer reading her rights to her and concentrated on what the persistent paramedic had said to Joseph. A bullet had grazed him. He needed a CT scan and a tetanus shot.

Instead of jail, he should have been brought to the hospital with Stacia. He needed someone to watch him overnight. And even though she could see that she was the last person he wanted to be around at the moment, she didn't intend to let him out of her sight again.

Less than an hour later, Elena pulled a blanket to Stacia's chin, having settled the child back into bed with her bedraggled white teddy bear at her side.

"I can't stop staring at her," she said, a sigh catching in her throat.

Strong hands closed over Elena's shoulders. "That's why you can't put her through anything else."

She uttered a soft sigh. "You heard David. The police *have* to talk to her."

"You can stall them for a while," he insisted. "You can get that social worker Ariel knows to say she's not up to talking yet."

She tore her gaze from her daughter and tipped her head back to meet his gaze. "Joseph—"

"Once the detectives finish investigating what we told them, along with the stuff David and Ty gave them that they already have on the murders and Donovan Roarke, we'll be cleared. You don't need to have anyone talk to her." His green eyes darkened with protectiveness.

"I don't want you to go to jail," she said. She didn't want him going anywhere, unless she was tucked in at his side, like Stacia and her teddy bear.

His fingers squeezed her shoulders, then released. "I won't. And neither will you."

She turned toward him, not needing his reassurance. She knew everything would be straightened out, her name and his cleared, whether Stacia had to testify or not. While she hated to put her little girl through anything else, Stacia was strong enough. She was far stronger than her mother and smarter because she had trusted Joseph, when she'd stepped off the catwalk and into his arms. The memory of her daughter's freefall chilled Elena, causing goose bumps to raise her skin and the hair at the nape of her neck.

She needed heat, the kind only Joseph could provide. With another glance at her daughter, who slept peacefully even in another strange bed, Elena stepped out of Joseph's guest room and into the hall. Despite having uninvited guests, he had been a gracious host, carrying Stacia, still groggy after being roused from Ariel's bed, upstairs.

She loved his place. It wasn't the type of house

she'd have expected the Joseph she had once thought he was to own. It wasn't cold and impersonal or rich and gaudy. The traditional brick colonial was solid and dependable, with big windows to let in lots of sunshine. It wasn't the kind of house a confirmed bachelor would own; it was a home in which a family could grow and play and live.

Now that she knew him, really knew him, she understood that this was exactly the kind of house Joseph would own. It represented everything he wanted but had never had. Could he put aside his hurt and anger to let her give it to him?

He opened the door of a room adjacent to the one in which Stacia slept. "You can sleep here," he offered.

"I wanted to come home with you to make sure you were okay," she said. Not to be tucked into some guest suite far away from him.

"You *insisted* on coming home with me," he reminded her. But he hadn't fought her that hard, their verbal struggle brief outside the police station. He'd even let her drive his SUV from the impound lot to the penthouse, and now back to his home. It wasn't far from the estate in terms of distance, but in warmth it was worlds apart from the house in which Elena had spent the past twenty years.

She couldn't go back there, not just because the police had declared it a crime scene, but because of all the bad memories. She'd taken with her the only good thing to ever come out of that house, Stacia. And she never intended to let her out of her sight again.

As Joseph leaned against the doorjamb and gazed back into Stacia's room, she realized he felt the same way.

"You two do have a special bond," she said, her voice soft so she wouldn't awaken her child.

He nodded. "Our little secret."

"I didn't realize how deep your bond was until she jumped into your arms."

He shuddered as if reliving that horrible moment, too. "It was almost as if she read my mind…."

Elena closed her eyes as a wave of emotion brought on fresh tears. "She did."

"That's her gift?"

"I think she has them all. She can see ghosts." She'd told Elena that Grandma Myra had been with her in the warehouse, before she and Joseph got there. "She can see the future."

"And she can read people's minds," Joseph said.

"God, I hope not everyone's," Elena said. "What if she read *his* mind…."

Joseph shook his head as he gazed into the

bedroom where Stacia lay. "No. She's sleeping too peacefully to know what *he's* thinking."

She reached out, sliding her fingers up the side of his face to where the bandage covered the wound at his temple. "I wish *you* could read *my* mind, Joseph."

He sighed as his hand closed around hers, pulling her fingers away from his face. "I don't need to, Elena. I know what I need to know. You don't trust me. If you did, you would have given *me* Roarke's cell number. You would never have gone behind my back to make your deal with the devil."

She shook her head. "You don't know the truth, Joseph."

Tugging on their joined hands, she pulled him toward the open door of the darkened bedroom. With her free hand, she fumbled for a switch and bathed the room in soft light. This wasn't just a spare guest room. The furniture was heavy, masculine, the bed already turned down, a man's robe tossed across the foot of it. This was his. Like she was.

His steps slow and reluctant, he followed her into the room, with its caramel-colored walls and rich oak trim. His throat moved as she closed the two-panel door behind them. "So what is the truth, Elena?"

"I couldn't sacrifice you for my daughter." And now she knew why. "I love you both."

His breath caught, then he harshly exhaled it.

"Elena, don't say something you don't mean, something in the heat of the moment—"

She reached up, brushing her mouth across his to silence him. Then she murmured, "It's okay. You don't have to love me back. Just hold me, Joseph, the way you hold me in my dreams…."

His arms, shaking slightly, closed around her, pulling her against the long, hard length of his body. His erection strained the fly of his suit pants and pushed against her hip. Maybe he didn't love her, but he desired her. "Elena—"

She didn't want his explanations or regrets. She wanted only him. She rose up on tiptoe again and pressed her lips to his. He kissed her hungrily, his mouth consuming hers with deep kisses, his tongue sliding in and out with delicious friction.

Her stomach clenched, as heat poured through her. With trembling fingers, she fumbled with the buttons on his shirt, parting it to reveal the hard, hair-dusted muscles of his chest.

He caught the hem of her sweater, pulling it up and over her head. Her hair drifted down, tangling around her shoulders. He dropped his hands and stepped back, breathing hard and fast through his mouth. "God, Elena, I can't—"

She reached up, running fingers through her hair. She had to look pretty horrible, dirty and bruised, from the ordeal in the warehouse. But still his rejection stung. She blinked back tears, and summoning her pride, lifted her chin.

He reached out again and stroked his fingers along her jaw. "You're so proud. So strong. I can't believe the way you fought for Stacia." His throat moved as he swallowed hard. "And for me."

"For us…" So that they might have a future they could envision together.

His thumb stroked over her lip, where it was swollen and cracked from Roarke's fist. "You're hurt. I can't hurt you any more."

"Then stay with me. Make love to me, Joseph," she pleaded, her pride be damned.

His fingers glided over her throat and shoulders, pushing her bra straps down her shoulders. "I don't deserve you."

She could argue with him all night, but she couldn't make him listen. She could make him *feel* though. She reached behind her, unclasping her bra so that it fell away. Then she stepped close to him, crushing her breasts against his chest, as she wound her arms around his back and held tight. "Make love to me, Joseph."

His lips lifted, just a fraction, as a smile teased them. "You're so bossy."

"Then do what I say."

His green eyes narrowed, he acknowledged, "I guess I do work for you now."

Since Thora was dead. Elena couldn't believe it yet. Maybe if she'd gone back to the house—but she never intended to do that. She wanted to stay right here…if Joseph wanted her.

From the way passion gleamed in his eyes, she suspected he wanted her now. But for always?

He bent his neck and leaned over, sliding his mouth along the territory his hands had covered, her jaw, her throat, the bare skin on her shoulders. She lifted her head, claiming his mouth with hers. Despite the cut and swelling on her lip, she felt no pain. Only love.

For Joseph. She'd worry about what he felt for her later. Her hands skimmed his back, the muscles rippling beneath her touch. Then he lifted her, carrying her to the bed. The chocolate-colored comforter soft beneath her back, Elena settled against the pile of pillows and watched as Joseph undid his belt and zipper. His pants dropped, revealing knit boxers, his erection straining against the dark blue cotton. Then that was gone too as he skimmed his underwear down his hips.

Elena's stomach clenched again, as heat pooled between her legs. She fumbled with the button on her borrowed jeans, only managing to open it and drag down the zipper before Joseph pulled the denim down her legs, leaving her naked but for a wisp of satin.

Joseph followed her down on the mattress, covering her body with his. Then, probably so she wouldn't bear the brunt of his weight, he rolled them. Skin brushed skin as limbs tangled. Soft hair on his legs and chest tickled her. She giggled, rejoicing in being alive, in being in his arms again. This afternoon she'd thought might be their last time together.

He took her mouth, claiming it with his lips and tongue, laving her cut with tenderness. Her breath sighed out, with relief and love. She'd never known she could feel so much, so deeply. "Joseph…"

His hands moved, stroking over every inch of her. He caressed her back, making her arch into his touch like a cat begging to be petted. He petted, stroking his hand down her back to her hips, then thighs.

She shifted her legs as heat coursed through her. He pushed her thighs apart, moving his hand between them. His fingers stroked over her wet core, again and again, until she cried out, an orgasm shuddering through her. "Joseph!"

Then she reached for him, closing her hand over the length of him. Up and down she stroked his long shaft while he buried his face in her neck. His teeth nipped at her earlobe, teasing it as she teased him. His breath sighed out, hot against her throat.

He caught her hand, stilling it. "Elena…"

"But I want to," she protested.

"We can't always have what we want," he said, sadness darkening his eyes. Obviously he'd been denied a lot growing up, not just financially but emotionally. He'd never had anyone in his life who really cared about him.

Until now.

And Elena intended to prove that to him. She leaned forward, closing her lips around the glistening tip of his penis.

Joseph groaned, as her lips imitated the earlier actions of her hand, sliding up and down as deep as she could take him in her throat. Then his hand fisted in her hair, pulling her back. "No," he told her, "I want to bury myself so deep inside you that you'll feel me forever as a part of you."

She shivered, as she lived the reality of one of the visions of the two of them together. Perhaps thinking her cold, perhaps just overcome with emotion, he covered her body with his. Then he dragged her legs up over his shoulders and buried himself deep inside her, just as he'd promised. Now, and in her dreams.

Elena met his thrusts as he pounded into her. Orgasm after orgasm rippled through her. She bit his shoulder to hold in her cries of pleasure. As her teeth nipped his skin, he uttered a guttural groan and pumped his own orgasm into her. Then, spent, he collapsed on top of her, his breath coming in harsh gasps.

Instead of being crushed by his weight, she felt cherished, protected. Safe, as she hadn't felt safe since the witch hunt began. No, longer than that. Safer than she'd felt in twenty years.

"I love you," she told, hoping this time that he believed her.

Instead of accepting her declaration, he stiffened and eased out of her, and off her, rolling to his side. He dragged his hands over his face and sighed.

"Joseph, why don't you believe me?" she asked, her heart aching with the love he refused to accept.

"You lied to me this afternoon. I knew something was going on. But you wouldn't tell me the truth. Even when we, when we did *this* then," he said, "it was like you were saying goodbye. Like it was the last time."

She bit her lip, then nodded. "I thought it might be. I didn't know what would happen—"

"You should have told me what you were up to, with Roarke. You should have trusted me, Elena."

"I do trust you, Joseph. I didn't want you getting hurt." She'd had that awful vision, the one of him lying dead on the floor, swimming in his own blood. She couldn't have borne that coming to pass. "I need you."

"Now," he agreed. "When you realized your plan of going it alone would have failed."

She shuddered and acknowledged, "You're right. I could have lost Stacia."

If not for Joseph catching her.

"And your own life," he pointed out. "He would have killed you both."

"I thought for the charms he might spare us," she explained. "Stacia and I are McGregors."

"You can't make a deal with a man like Roarke. He's crazy. And dangerous."

She couldn't argue with him about that, only about her love. "Joseph—"

But he refused to listen. "You're scared for your safety and Stacia's. But what about when Roarke is caught and put behind bars? Will you need me then?"

"Joseph—"

"I want you and Stacia to stay here, with me, so I can make sure you're safe. So I can sleep nights knowing that Roarke won't get to you. But after that…"

He'd throw them out? Before Elena could ask, he slipped from the bed, threw on his robe, and walked out.

Maybe it was time she faced the fact that he didn't love her. Felicia's sister had called her cold, saying that she'd frozen Kirk out of her life. Maybe she had. And maybe Joseph feared she'd do the same to him.

Exhausted, both physically and emotionally, she fell asleep, never knowing if he came back to bed.

Joseph watched her sleep, unable to believe that she was really in his bed, in his life…even if it were just until Roarke was caught. She only *thought* she loved him. But he couldn't hold her to what she said now, when she was afraid for her life and her daughter's.

He tucked Stacia under his arm, his fingers gently poking into her side until she squirmed and giggled. "Shhh, you're going to wake your mother."

"Too late," Elena murmured, as she stretched and reached up for her daughter. Some time in the night she must have found the nightshirt he'd laid out for her. She wore it now, the blue silk bringing out the vibrant color of her eyes. "Hey, baby, I missed you."

Stacia snuggled close, her arms tight around her mother's neck. She blew out a soft breath. "I had a dream. Joseph heard me and woke me up."

Elena tensed. "Was it another bad dream, honey?"

He'd thought the same when he'd heard the child murmuring in her sleep. He hadn't wanted her to relive any of the horror she'd experienced the past couple of days. They'd have to find another way to clear themselves; Stacia would only testify over his dead body.

The little girl shook her head. "Nope. It was a good one."

Elena's mouth eased into a relieved smile, splitting her lip again where Roarke had hit her. Joseph's gut tightened. He had to get hold of that man; he had to hurt him like he'd hurt Elena and Stacia.

Stacia stood up on the bed and threw herself back into Joseph's arms. "You don't have to worry," she told him. "He's not going to come after us again."

"What?" She'd known what he was thinking. His mouth quirked into a grin. She really had all the gifts.

"He knows you'll protect us, Joseph. He knows he can't get to us now. My dream was about living here, you, me and Mommy, as a family. A real family."

Not the one she'd had with her father always being gone. Joseph knew what she wanted. He'd wanted it himself growing up. God, when Roarke was caught and Elena left, he wasn't the only one who'd get hurt.

"I'm going to leave you two alone for a while," he said, his throat thick with emotion. "I'll make some calls…."

And get them out of his house and out of his life before anyone got hurt any more.

Elena winced as the door shut behind Joseph's back, not at the sound. The click as the door hit the jamb was barely audible. Her discomfort was in watching him walk away from her again. He didn't love her. She needed to finally accept that.

A little hand cradled Elena's cheek. "Mommy, Joseph loves you. He's loved you for a long time."

Elena's heart swelled with hope. "You can really read his mind?"

Stacia nodded. "That's how I knew to jump into his arms. I knew he'd catch me." Her mouth pulled into a frown, and her pale blue eyes shimmered with tears. "Daddy wouldn't have caught me. He took me away because he was trying to save me, because I told him about the dreams and the ghosts, and he was scared." Her breath caught as she admitted the truth about her father. "For himself. Joseph's scared for *us,* Mommy. He really loves us."

"And you know this because you've heard his thoughts?"

Stacia nodded. "Like I see ghosts."

"And have visions. Do you know what that makes you?" Not cursed. She didn't want Stacia persecuted for her gift as Thora had persecuted Elena for so many years.

Stacia nodded again and answered matter-of-factly, "A witch."

Elena's heart thumped hard. "Did the bad man call you that?"

"Yes. He said it like it's a bad thing." Her blue eyes earnest, Stacia continued, "But it's not. Being a witch is a good thing, Mommy. I can help people."

"When you're older," Elena added the qualifier. "You can use your gifts." Instead of denying them like Elena had done for so long. She wasn't about to deny herself any longer.

"I'm really tired," Stacia said. "I'm going to lay back down with Teddy. I don't like leaving him alone."

But she wanted to leave Elena alone…to talk to Joseph. He'd stepped back into the room, his gaze steady on her little girl. "Everything all right?" he asked.

Stacia nodded. "I'm just tired."

"Want me to tuck you back in?"

She shook her head. "It's okay. I know where my bed is."

Elena almost smiled. Did he realize her little girl had staked claim on his house, on him?

He didn't speak until the door closed behind her, then he said, "At least she won't have to go through anything else. Koster called. The police accepted our story. They actually were watching the house, waiting for you, when Roarke killed

Thora. Since it's the same gun that killed Kirk and Felicia, we're cleared."

"Is that all David told you?" she asked, curious about how tightly he clenched his jaw when he should have been relieved. Not just because of their freedom but because Stacia wouldn't have to relive her ordeal. He'd been more concerned about that than she'd been. Stacia was strong; she would never deny who and what she was.

Joseph shook his head. "He said you and Stacia can stay with him and Ariel, at the penthouse, until Roarke's caught. He's already upped the security there."

"Joseph…"

"You told her already, anyhow," he said, gesturing toward the closed door.

"Told Stacia what?"

"That her dream isn't going to come true." His voice deepened with emotion. "We're not going to be that little happy family she wants."

Elena blinked at him, as if she hadn't heard him right. "Why would I tell her that?"

His eyes darkened with disappointment. "I didn't think you'd lie to *her*."

"I'm not lying, Joseph. I love you. I want to stay here, even after Roarke is caught."

He sighed and pushed a shaking hand through

his hair. "Come on, Elena. We both know I'm not *that* guy."

"What guy?" And then she realized why he kept walking away: so he could do it first. He was convinced that like everyone else in his life, the father he'd never known, the mother who'd thrown him out, she would leave him.

"That family guy," he said, as if he spoke again of the white knight he'd claimed he'd never be for her even though he'd rescued her and her daughter. "The husband. The father. How can I be what I've never known?"

"Instinct," she said, shrugging. "I don't know. You've already been more for me than my husband was, more for Stacia than her father was. You're the man we need, Joseph."

"For now," he agreed, his throat raw with the emotions he fought.

Her hope burgeoned. Stacia was right. He did love her.

"I *need* you, Joseph. Not to protect me. I need you because my love for you makes *me* strong. For the first time in my life, I'm brave enough to fight for what I want. I want you. Not just until Roarke is caught but forever."

She stopped to drag in a necessary breath. "Share my vision of the future with me, with me *and* Stacia."

His green eyes glistened as the emotions consumed him. "Elena, I won't be able to handle it if you leave, if you walk out of my life and take that special little girl with you. I won't be able to—"

She stood on the bed, like her daughter had, and catapulted herself into his arms. "You won't have to handle anything, Joseph, but happiness. I'm never leaving you."

He drew in a shaky breath, as he buried his face in her neck. "I love you so much, Elena."

Her heart lurched as she accepted the gift he'd given her, words he'd never spoken to anyone before her. Tears burned her eyes, not tears of fear or pain; she'd shed so many of those since the witch hunt began. Now she wept tears of happiness. Of hope for the future she knew she'd have, with her little girl and the man she loved.

"I love you, Joseph. I'll love you forever."

Epilogue

She was the one. The only witch he could kill.

The others knew about the witch hunt. They were united and protected and far more powerful than they'd been before. They were using their gifts and the charms and the men who loved them.

Fools, the men who'd fallen so deeply under the witches' spells that they'd risked their lives for them. They'd gotten in his way, disrupted his plans. He wouldn't have that problem with her. She was all alone.

Even with all their power, the witches hadn't been able to find her, their little sister.

No one knew where Irina Cooper was. No one but him.

He was a damned good private investigator. He had connections and sources, and he'd called in every favor owed him to learn her new identity and find her. But even then tracking her down hadn't been easy.

She wasn't like her sisters. She had no idea who or what she was. So she'd lost her mind.

He didn't care. He didn't want her mind. He wanted her charm, and her life.

* * * * *

Don't miss Damned, *the third book in Lisa Child's thrilling WITCH HUNT mini-series, available in October 2008 wherever Mills & Boon® books are sold.*

*Mills & Boon® Intrigue
brings you a sneak preview of…*

Delores Fossen's Whose Baby?

*Kelly Manning is stunned to learn that her infant
might have been switched at birth with another.
To get the truth means getting at single father
Nick Lattimer, a Renaissance cowboy deep in a
family struggle over a lavish Texan ranch.*

*Don't miss the fantastic second story in the
heart-warming* FOR THEIR BABY'S SAKE
*series, available next month in
Mills & Boon® Intrigue!*

Whose Baby?
by
Delores Fossen

Bexar County, Texas

Kelly Manning checked to make sure no one was following her. No one was. She was alone in the dimly lit hallway.

So far, so good.

Too bad her pounding heart and racing breath didn't quite grasp that she was close to succeeding. A minute, maybe less, and she'd have what she needed and would be away from Nick Lattimer's ranch.

Of course, this could be just the beginning. Not exactly a comforting thought, but she would cross that bridge *if* she came to it. However, it was impossible to push aside the thought that the next few minutes could change her life forever.

She eased open the door to the nursery and ducked inside. The nanny was in the kitchen indulging in a late-night snack, so other than the baby, the suite would be empty. Timing was indeed everything. If any of the half-dozen or so "security guards" and household staff caught her, they would no doubt alert their boss.

Definitely not good.

Kelly hurried across the room to the crib. The baby was there. Sleeping. He was tucked beneath a blue satin-rimmed blanket. All she could see of him was the mop of blondish-brown hair, but with just that bit of visual info, she had to fight to hold on to her breath. Now wasn't the time to let her emotions get in the way of what she had to do.

With her hands trembling, she reached for the small vial she'd hidden in her bra. But reaching for it was as far as she got.

"Mind telling me what you're doing here?" she heard someone ask.

The sound shot through her entire body, and Kelly gasped. She didn't recognize the voice, but she had no doubt that it belonged to Nick Lattimer, the lord of the massive Texas ranch she was trespassing on. And he was the last person on earth she wanted to come face-to-face with tonight.

Heaven help her.

Dreading what she would see, Kelly angled her eyes in the direction of his voice. He was in the shadows, his shoulder resting against the doorjamb of the adjoining room. His head was slightly tilted to the side. Studying her. He wore a tux and a formidable take-no-prisoners expression.

"I was looking for the ladies' room," she managed to say. She'd practiced it enough that thankfully her voice didn't crack.

He pushed away from the doorjamb, a slick effortless move, and he started toward her. A pair of delicate angel night-lights illuminated his way. Ironic, since there was nothing angelic or delicate about him.

His midnight-black hair fell long and fashionably untamed against his neck. Dark, brooding eyes. Chiseled jaw. High cheekbones that hinted of Native American blood. He was handsome by anyone's standards.

Including hers, much to her disgust.

But his looks didn't make him less dangerous. From all accounts, he was an ends-justifies-the-means sort of man. *Any means.*

"The caterer and party staff were instructed to use the downstairs facilities," he informed her.

Kelly nodded. "I'm sorry, sir. I didn't know that." She turned to walk away.

Nick Lattimer shifted to the side and blocked her exit. He didn't stop there. He blocked her a second time when she tried to go around him. Then he circled her. Slowly. Like a hungry jungle cat stalking his prey.

Outside the window, lightning stabbed across the sky, quickly followed by thunder. The November storm only added to the menacing energy simmering around him.

"I wasn't joking about having to go to the ladies' room." Kelly tried to keep her tone light. She failed. Her heart was beating so hard and fast that she thought her ribs might crack.

He was behind her when she heard the whisper-soft sound. She might not have even known what it was. But she was a cop's widow.

It was a gun.

Oh, mercy.

It'd been a serious mistake coming here, but it was too late to turn back.

She got a good look at the weapon as he finished circling her and came to a standstill directly in front of her. Yes, it was definitely a gun. An expensive, high-powered Glock. Not an amateur's weapon of choice. It was too much to hope that he didn't know how to use it.

Her stomach tightened into a cold, hard knot.

Kelly forced herself not to panic. The stakes were too high for her to lose it. "Listen, I've obviously upset you by being here. It won't happen again."

"I don't doubt that. Only a handful of people have ever managed to upset me more than once." His narrowed gaze slid over her. "Who sent you?"

She'd anticipated a lot of questions. But not that one. Kelly shook her head. "What do you mean?"

"I mean… Who. Sent. You?"

Okay. It was clear from his sarcastic tone that he had his own issues and wouldn't let her just walk out. It was time to show a little backbone.

She hiked up her chin. "I understood what you said, but I thought the answer was obvious. I work for the caterer you hired for your dinner party." She pointed to her clothes. "You didn't think I was wearing this tacky polyester uniform to make a fashion statement, did you?"

"No. But it did occur to me that you were wearing it so you could gain access to my home. And to this particular room."

Without taking his lethal gaze off her, he reached out, snagged her by the shoulder and pushed her against the wall. Her right cheek landed next to a cheery cherub mural.

Other than a startled sound of protest, Kelly didn't have time to react before his left hand was on her. Moving across her back. To her sides. And her stomach. She battled with her instincts to fight back. But this wasn't a fight she could win. Not with his size and that Glock. Maybe once he realized she wasn't armed, he'd back off. Of course, he might find the vial. Even so, he likely wouldn't know what it was.

"So, is this how you treat your hired help?" Kelly snarled.

"It is when I find them in places they shouldn't be."

That searching hand went lower, to the stretchy waist of her dark-blue skirt. And even lower. He slid his palm along the outside of her legs. Then, the inside.

All the way up.

When his fingers made it to the lower front of her panties, Kelly grabbed his wrist and clamped onto his hand. Too bad she hadn't opted to wear her sturdy cotton underwear. Or her big-girl panties, as her grandmother used to call them. Instead, she had a little swatch of silk and lace that allowed her to feel every inch of his touch.

A touch she didn't want to feel.

She glared at him over her shoulder. "This isn't necessary."

"Oh, but it is," he countered.

Kelly had stopped his search in her panty region. Not the best idea she had ever had. Maybe it was her grip on his wrist, or maybe he was just a jerk—either way, he kept his hand there.

"Look, if this is your idea of foreplay—"

"It isn't." He threw off her grip and resumed his search. "Trust me, if it were foreplay, at least one of us would be enjoying it."

Apparently finished with the zinging smart-aleck comebacks and the search of her midsection, he caught on to her shoulder and whirled her around to face him. Kelly had to look up to meet him eye to eye. She was five-six, and he had a good seven inches on her. Plus, there was the weight difference. He outsized her by sixty pounds or more.

All muscle, no doubt.

He didn't look like the excessive-body-fat type. His size and strength would be a definite liability if she had to fight her way out of there.

Unfortunately, she might not have a choice about that.

"Were you trying to kidnap the baby?" Lattimer demanded.

That didn't do much to ease the knot in her stomach. Whatever she'd been expecting him to say, that wasn't it. "No! Absolutely not."

"Good. Because you would have failed."

Celebrate 100 years of pure reading pleasure with Mills & Boon®

To mark our centenary, each month we're publishing a special 100th Birthday Edition. These celebratory editions are packed with extra features and include a FREE bonus story.

Plus, you have the chance to enter a fabulous monthly prize draw. See 100th Birthday Edition books for details.

Now that's worth celebrating!

September 2008

Crazy about her Spanish Boss by Rebecca Winters
Includes FREE bonus story
Rafael's Convenient Proposal

November 2008

**The Rancher's Christmas Baby
by Cathy Gillen Thacker**
Includes FREE bonus story *Baby's First Christmas*

December 2008

One Magical Christmas by Carol Marinelli
Includes FREE bonus story *Emergency at Bayside*

Look for Mills & Boon® 100th Birthday Editions at your favourite bookseller or visit
www.millsandboon.co.uk

FREE!

4 Books
and a surprise gift!

We would like to take this opportunity to thank you for reading this Mills & Boon® book by offering you the chance to take FOUR more specially selected titles from the Intrigue series absolutely FREE! We're also making this offer to introduce you to the benefits of the Mills & Boon® Book Club—

- ★ FREE home delivery
- ★ FREE gifts and competitions
- ★ FREE monthly Newsletter
- ★ Exclusive Mills & Boon Book Club offers
- ★ Books available before they're in the shops

Accepting these FREE books and gift places you under no obligation to buy, you may cancel at any time, even after receiving your free shipment. Simply complete your details below and return the entire page to the address below. You don't even need a stamp!

YES! Please send me 4 free Intrigue books and a surprise gift. I understand that unless you hear from me, I will receive 6 superb new titles every month for just £3.15 each, postage and packing free. I am under no obligation to purchase any books and may cancel my subscription at any time. The free books and gift will be mine to keep in any case.

18ZEF

Ms/Mrs/Miss/Mr ....Initials ....

BLOCK CAPITALS PLEASE

Surname ....

Address ....

....

....Postcode ....

Send this whole page to:
UK: FREEPOST CN81, Croydon, CR9 3WZ